Fiction
Housholder
David

Housholder, David

The Blackberry
Bush.

JUL 1 5 2011

D0401644

Some books make you silent.
Some books give you goosebumps.
Some books change your life.
The Blackberry Bush…it's one of those books…read it!

> —**Geert Kimpen,** *best-selling European fiction author*
> *of* De Geheime Newton

A delightful blend of the historical events of the twentieth
century and the coming of age of young people, both physically
and spiritually. You'll come away feeling more spiritual, believing
in angels, and that good trumps evil. This book will lift your heart
and fill you with hope!

> —**Ralph Moore,** *Founder of the Hope Chapel Movement*

I live in this book and care desperately for these people.

> —**Dana Hanson,** *Pastor, LIFEhouse Church (Los Angeles)*

David Housholder cooks up a great stew in his novel *The
Blackberry Bush*. He mixes Old Europe, contemporary California,
international headlines, youthful passion, and Christian
spirituality to create a story that warms the heart and forces you
to think about who you are, where you came from, and why life is
never, ever accidental.

> —**J. Lee Grady,** *author and journalist*

The Blackberry Bush proves that there really is more to life than what we see on the surface.

—**TAMMY DUNAHOO,** *General Supervisor,*
The Foursquare Church

Housholder delivers a gripping, globetrotting, multicultural story—one populated by real people caught up in forces they could not possibly comprehend who find redemption and meaning through a personal encounter with a spiritual reality beyond themselves. *The Blackberry Bush* will show you the way out of your own thorny thickets of life into a place of genuine spiritual freedom.

—**BOB ROGNLIEN,** *Senior Pastor, Lutheran Church*
of the Good Shepherd (Torrance, California) and author
of Experiential Worship

With his novel *The Blackberry Bush* David Housholder has given us a brilliant work of coming-of-age fiction that not only captures and holds the attention of the reader, but seduces us into an exploration of the possibilities of hope and meaning in a vacuous and spiritually bankrupt world.

—**BRIAN ZAHND,** *Senior Pastor, Word of Life Church*
(St. Joseph, Missouri) and author of Unconditional?

THE

BLACKBERRY

BUSH

DAVID HOUSHOLDER

summerside
PRESS™

Summerside Press™
Minneapolis 55337
www.summersidepress.com

The Blackberry Bush
© 2011 by David Housholder

ISBN 978-1-60936-116-7

All rights reserved. No part of this book may be reproduced in any form, except for brief quotations in printed reviews, without permission in writing from the publisher.

English Scripture references are from the King James Version of the Bible.

"*De afgrond roept tot den afgrond.*" From the Dutch Staten Vertaling of the Bible, 1635. Psalm 42.

"*Jesu, HERR, gedenke an mich, wenn du in dein Reich kommst!*" From Martin Luther's German translation of the Bible, 1545.

Cover design by Faceout Studios, Charles Brock
Cover photo © Paul Knight/Trevillion Images
Author photos © Shannon McMannus
Interior Design by Müllerhaus Publishing Group | www.mullerhaus.net

Edited by Ramona Cramer Tucker

Some locations depicted in this book are real places, but the story is entirely fictional. All resemblances to actual people (other than ones noted in the author's acknowledgments) are purely coincidental.

Summerside Press™ is an inspirational publisher offering fresh, irresistible books to uplift the heart and engage the mind.

Printed in Canada

For
Marinus Vermeer and J. E. Danielson,
whom my wife, Wendy, and I miss a great deal.
We are still carrying their torches.

ACKNOWLEDGMENTS

Thanks to everyone, and there are hundreds of you, who made this first novel of the series possible. A novel is a quilt with many borrowed insights and ideas.

Props to Rolf and Mary Garborg at Summerside Press, who believed in me and got this project going, and their superlative next generation team of Carlton, Jason, and Joanie, who together with others lead Summerside Press.

No character in this novel correlates to a person in the "real world" except for two. Gemechis and Lindsey are delightful characters that appear briefly in the epilogue and are indeed based wholly on two fascinating real people: Gemechis Buba and Lindsey Trego. Some celebrities and public figures do appear in the book, either in passing or as cameos, but that's only to keep the story stapled to the real world in which Josh and Kati grew up.

All the rest are composite characters based on at least a half dozen tiny bits and pieces of people I've observed over the years. Their names have nothing to do with real people. So, if you see yourself in this book, well, you're seeing things.

Thanks to my wife, Wendy, who thinks I can do anything. That helps a lot. More than you think.

Thanks to Steffen Kopetzky, writer of one of my fave novels, *Grand Tour.* One of the main characters from his book, the mythic Ziffer watch, needed a bit of a resurrection. It was too good to leave in literary limbo.

Blessings on David and Linda Housholder (no relation, remarkably), who lived in South Asia for a full generation and gave me the ideas for Zara's family.

Thanks to Robinwood Church of Huntington Beach, California (RobinwoodChurch.com), which provided the venue over the years for developing the spiritual themes underlying the story. This indie-warehouse-beach-church has a heart for changing the world. We probably will—because we believe we can. We have a worldwide following on iTunes podcasts. Have a listen.

Thanks to the wonderful folks at Hope Lutheran Church on Melrose in LA for hosting some of the most important scenes of the story. Ditto for the Evangelische Gemeinde Oberwinter in Germany and the Hillegonda Kerk in Hillegersberg, Holland. Please visit all these churches on Sunday morning if you are nearby. The latter two churches have been torch-carriers for many, many generations.

Thanks to my wonderful test-readers: Justin Burtis, Addie Coffman, Peter Stevens, Lindsey Trego, Luke Allison, and Madi Hankins.

Thanks to Ramona Tucker, editorial athlete, who created lucidity and clarity out of...well...my writing. She also provided many of the plot ideas.

Thanks to Ken Blanchard, of *The One Minute Manager,* who convinced me to start writing a couple of years ago.

Thanks most of all to that baritone voice Kati describes in the epilogue of this novel. Compared to him, the rest of us are just footnoters.

And thanks to Jim Rosenthal, who used to eat wild blackberries with me while on jogging runs outside of Chimacum, Washington.

FOREWORD

Sooner or later in life we all discover that something in us is broken—and that there's an empty void we want filled with pure, unconditional love and acceptance. We all long for a way out of the trap of meaninglessness…a way to be reborn into a new life of purpose and freedom.

The Blackberry Bush is a beautifully written novel of two characters' search for meaning and their powerful rescue from the relational and societal expectations that are crushing them. It's the story our own hearts might tell from our journey through life.

I identified most with the character of Kati. Like her, I eventually heard God's voice after going through some difficult years with bullies and people who couldn't accept me as I was. I had to discover and accept the truth that all of me—my past, my relationships, my experiences, and gifts—is meant to be used for a purpose larger than just myself. David Housholder also reveals the importance of our backstories—the legacies from our parents, grandparents, and great-grandparents that influence who we are and what we become. It was an encouragement to me to look at both painful and fortuitous events from my past as I work to weave past, present, and future into a whole.

But I also found myself embracing Josh's words of truth: "Only by abandoning all attempts to meet others' expectations can you truly hear the voice of the Spirit and be freed to pursue what God would have you uniquely do."

As the wise apostle Paul says in 2 Corinthians 3, we can be free of all this stuff. All of it! And when we are, nothing stands between us and God. Then our faces can shine with the reflection of his light, and our lives gradually become more and more beautiful.

May this gripping story—spanning generations and continents—provide entertainment, reflection, and new direction for your life, so you too may move ahead into the light of freedom and joy.

Debbie Griffith

DEBBIE GRIFFITH, *speaker and radio host of "Everyday Matters," is also a contributor to Focus on the Family's TV Ministry "Your Family Live."*

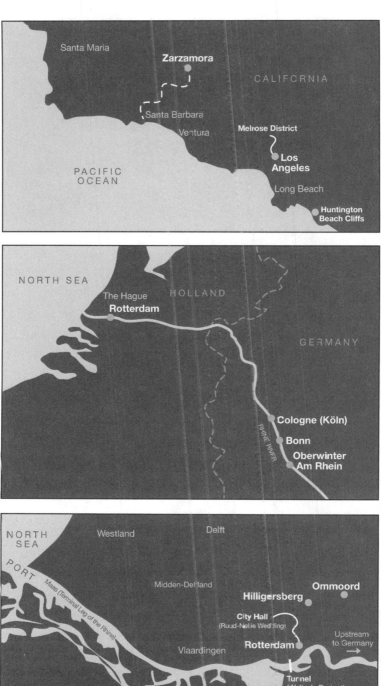

THE GENERATIONS

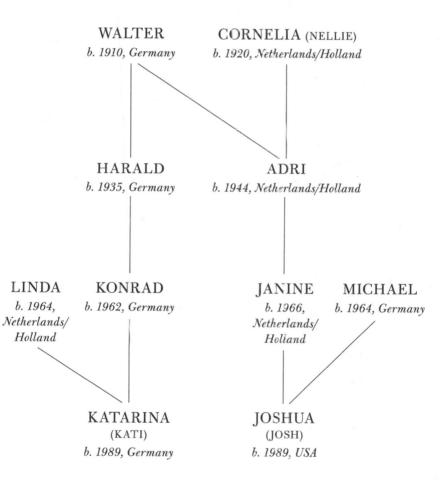

WALTER
b. 1910, Germany

CORNELIA (NELLIE)
b. 1920, Netherlands/Holland

HARALD
b. 1935, Germany

ADRI
b. 1944, Netherlands/Holland

LINDA
b. 1964,
Netherlands/
Holland

KONRAD
b. 1962, Germany

JANINE
b. 1966,
Netherlands/
Holland

MICHAEL
b. 1964, Germany

KATARINA
(KATI)
b. 1989, Germany

JOSHUA
(JOSH)
b. 1989, USA

Think for a moment. Isn't there a splendid randomness to the way your day is coming together today?

After all, it's not the big, dramatic things we foresee and expect that make all the difference in our lives. It's the chance, random encounters—the subtle things that surprise us…and change the very course of our individual destinies.

The Blackberry Bush is a story about awakening to the fullness of this reality.

And you will never want to go back to sleep.

You can call me Angelo. I'll be the one telling this story. As you and I travel together across generations and continents in a journey that will take just a few hours, you'll discover not only the gripping stories of Kati, Josh, Walter, Nellie, and Janine but also uncover your own compelling backstory that will change you in ways you can never imagine.

And you'll never be the same again.…

PROLOGUE

1989

Berlin, Germany

OCCASIONALLY, OUT OF NOWHERE, history turns on a dime in a way no one sees coming. Listen...do you hear the sound of jackhammers on dirty concrete?

"*Wir sind ein Volk* (We are one people)!" A large European outdoor crowd chants this over and over into the chilly November night. "*Wir sind ein Volk!*"

Thousands of hands hold candles high in the darkening night of Berlin. Throngs of young people with brightly colored scarves crowd the open spaces between concrete buildings. There are parties—with exuberant celebrants of all ages—even along the actual top of the wall. Flowers are stuffed into once-lethal Kalashnikov rifles. Hope is contagious.

It's November 9, 1989. The first sections of the Berlin Wall are removed, to mass cheers, with heavy machinery. It seems incomprehensible that a small weekly Monday prayer meeting in Pastor Magerius's Leipzig, Germany, study grew into the pews of the Nicolai Church and eventually out into the Leipzig city square. Then today, this "Peace Prayer," figuratively speaking, traveled up the Autobahn to Berlin and converged as an army of liberation on that iconic concrete symbol of Cold War division—with world-news cameras whirring.

Little things can make a big difference. Subtle potency. Gentle power.

"*Wir sind ein Volk*," the crowd chants as one.

The Berlin Wall—a filthy, gravity-based ring of rebar and concrete, tangled with barbed wire and patrolled by German shepherd attack dogs–has encircled and separated West from East for twenty-eight years. Now it is irreparably pierced.

Unthinkable. No one saw this coming.

Walls are real, you see, yet they always come down. Creation and nature never favor walls. They start to crumble, even before the mortar dries.

*

Elisabeth Hospital
Bonn, Germany
A day's Autobahn drive from the festivities in Berlin

THAT SAME INSTANT, a severely pregnant woman's water breaks in the tall-windowed birthing room of the Elisabeth Hospital in Bonn, Germany.

Hours later: "*Ein Mädchen* (a girl)!" *Een meisje,* translates the exhausted mother with silently moving lips into her native Dutch. Linda, a sojourner in Germany, was born a generation ago in Holland.

Mere blocks away from the birth scene, the mighty Rhine River flows past Bonn on its way downstream to the massive industrial port city of Rotterdam, Linda's hometown. Only a few hours away by river barge, Rotterdam, Holland, couldn't be farther from Germany—on so many levels.

The labor has been long and brutally hard. The father, Konrad, takes little newborn, black-haired Katarina up the elevator to the nursery. On the way up, an old woman in a wheelchair spontaneously pronounces God's blessing over baby "Kati" (pronounced "KAH-tee," in the German way) with the sign of the cross. Kati focuses her glassy little eyes on the woman's wristwatch.

Konrad is concerned about how pale Katarina is. Was her older sister, Johanna, this porcelain-skinned at birth? Perhaps it's the thick shock of black hair that sharpens the contrast with her complexion. *How will Kati and Johanna get along?* he wonders. *I guess that will all start to unfold soon, when they meet each other for the first time.*

I won't be able to protect her, thinks Konrad. Parental anxiety starts creeping up his spine in ways it never did when Johanna, now two, was born.

Perhaps little Kati will need that elevator blessing, he muses uncomfortably.

*

Zarzamora, California
1989

ANOTHER WOMAN WITH ROTTERDAM BLOODLINES, across the planet in sunny Zarzamora, California, is giving birth at the very same moment (although earlier in the day because of the time difference) to a boy. The tiny flat-roofed hospital up in the mountains of the Los Padres forest is the port of entry for little baby Joshua.

Janine smiles up at husband, Michael, and takes a first look at Josh, expecting, for whatever reason, to see a pale baby girl. Genuinely surprised—after all, this is in the days before ultrasound was universal—to see a vibrant, reddish-hued boy, she suppresses a giggle of delight, a catharsis of joy after so many miscarriages. What fun they will have together! Will he lighten up her melancholy disposition, perhaps?

Janine sighs in relief as she confirms to herself, *We're not going to have to take care of him much. He's going to be okay. I'm sure of it. I can tell.*

The trumpets of the practicing local high school marching band waft through the open windows as German-born father Michael washes his son off in the sink of the delivery room. The piercing eyes of baby Josh, almost white-blue, glisten in the overhead lights. They stop to focus on Michael for a fleeting minute, then zero in on some yet unseen reality behind his father's shoulder.

Shouldn't I be saying some ancient German words, a blessing or something, while I'm doing this? Michael asks himself.

But he can't think of any. He is adrift in the flowing current of this new experience.

The marching band plays on outside. *Are they really circling the hospital, or does it just sound like that?* the new father thinks....

~ Behind the Story ~
Angelo

I can watch both births as I pick and eat blackberries from the thicket back in rainy Bonn. I smile. Joshua looks so happy to be here. He radiates physical warmth and doesn't seem to need his blanket. He welcomes the new climate.

But Kati doesn't like the cold. There's almost a 30-degree (Fahrenheit) difference in ambient temperature from the womb to the room, and I see her struggle.

And then there's the brand-new "breathing" thing. How can breathing go from unnecessary to essential in a few seconds? Yet some days we don't even think about breathing, not even once. Amazing.

Joshua's American birth certificate reads *11-09-1989*. Kati's European one reads *09-11-1989*.

How much of their lives are preprogrammed? How much of their minds will be stamped with the thoughts of others? Is life a roll of the dice, or is it a script we just read out to the end? Don't we all wonder that same thing sometimes?

As Kati and Joshua start to adjust to life outside the womb, the Berlin Wall continues to crumble to shouts of joy.

I write the names *Linda and Konrad in Germany, Janine and Michael in California* on the inside of the book cover I'm holding. I always do that, so I don't get confused about who's who as I travel through their stories.

Both fathers, Konrad and Michael, have roots in the Germany

that was rebuilding after World War II. Both are self-doubting, somewhat weak Rheinlanders married to practical, sober, very Protestant Dutch women.

Katarina and Joshua are on parallel paths. But only *perfectly* parallel paths never meet as they stretch into infinity. And since these paths, like ours, aren't perfect...well, you can guess what might happen in this story.

Kati and Josh, born on one of the greatest days of freedom for all humankind, will grow up snared in the blackberry bush...like you.

But if you dare to engage their story at a heart level, a fresh new freedom might just be birthed in you.

So why not listen to that subtle twitter of conception inside your soul? The one that says, *This year something exciting is going to happen that I can't anticipate. And I'll never be the same....*

PART ONE

1999
Oberwinter am Rhein, Germany
Just south of Bonn

Kati

I LOVE LOOKING OUT our back picture window at the rolling farms. I'm watching for Opa, my dear grandfather Harald, who said he'd be home by 4 p.m. We live at the top of the road that winds uphill from the ancient Rhine River town of Oberwinter, just upstream from Bonn. That's how everybody here writes it, but they say ⸢Ova-venta." I walk up and down the sidewalk along the switchback road almost every day.

Our home is perched at the top of the hill with the front of the house facing the street that skirts the skyline of the ridge and the back looking away from the river, out at the plateau of peaceful farms, which Opa says the ancient Romans probably worked.

Opa knows a lot of secrets. If he told me what he knows every day for the rest of my life, he'd never run out of things to say. But sometimes he gets sad. He never likes to talk about how things were when he was my age. His voice starts to sound shaky, and that makes me sad too. I stopped asking him about his wartime childhood a long time ago.

My watch says it's another hour to wait. Really, it's his watch, big on my wrist. The leather band smells like Opa. I'm very careful with it since it's a Glashütte, which is infinitely special.

Sometimes Opa shows me his watch collection from the big mahogany box that's a lot like Mutti's (that's what I call my mother) silverware holder. But the Glashütte was always my favorite, and one day he gave it to me. I've worn it ever since.

Mutti was angry at Opa for giving it to me. "It's worth as much as a car!" she said. But Opa simply smiled. He never minds when people are upset with him.

Opa's study is a magical place. In the corner is the totem pole he brought home from Alaska. The wooden desk is covered with a sheet of glass. Under the glass are certificates, pictures of Opa shaking hands with people in suits and, right in the middle, a recent picture of me. The books on his shelves are in English and German. He has me read aloud from the chair across the desk from his and tells me that I speak English without an accent, just as they speak it in Seattle, Washington, where he worked for a few years. We're on our second time through Dale Carnegie's *How to Win Friends and Influence People*. Opa says it's a very important book, so I believe him.

Opa is the only one who doesn't seem worried about me. He never seems worried about anything. I can't remember seeing him angry. Ever.

I hope he takes me out to his workshop in the shed this evening. It's my favorite place. My big sister, Johanna, says it's not fun for girls, but she's wrong. Opa has hand tools and power tools, and all of them are perfectly hung and positioned. The shed is as clean as Mutti's kitchen.

Opa tells me that the Bible says all people have "gifts" from God and that all the gifts are open to girls as well as boys. He tells me I have the gifts of *craftsmanship* and *interpretation*. Those are big words, but they make me feel good.

We've made and fixed so many things together there. I have my own safety glasses. He lets me run the band saw all by myself. I can tell by looking at his eyes that he knows I'll be safe. Mutti doesn't have the same look in her eyes, no matter what I'm doing.

Mutti cuts my hair really short because she's afraid it's going to get caught in one of the power tools. I hate how it looks. She also tries, continually, to get me to eat more. She doesn't like how skinny I am.

Papa works in Berlin. He got transferred there when the German government moved from Bonn after the Wall fell, when I was little. He comes home on the train most weekends. He works for the foreign diplomatic service, and he told me this month that he might get transferred again soon, and that we might have to move to America. He and Mutti have been arguing a lot about it while I try to get to sleep at night.

I can tell the arguments are bad, because Mutti slips back into Dutch when she gets angry and also when she talks to me and Johanna. Anger and parenting seem to come out of the same place inside her.

Mutti, unlike Opa, loves to talk about growing up, and how wonderful everything was then. It's fun to hear the stories—and to see her smile while she tells them. We take the train to visit her Dutch parents often. It takes only a few hours to reach Rotterdam. I love riding through Cologne, past the blackened dual-spired cathedral. I have another grandfather in Holland who is kind of funny and crabby at the same time. I only have one grandmother, because my German Oma died of cancer before I was born.

I love Rotterdam. My Dutch grandfather (my other Opa) takes me on bike rides through the tunnel, under the big river, and to my favorite place—the Hotel New York in the heart of the port. He buys me a chocolate milk every time, and we watch the big ships come and go. He doesn't like to talk about Germans, even though he reminds me that they built the bike tunnel and highway under the river. Every now and then someone mentions the War. I've always known my

Dutch grandparents don't like my father. They say it's not because Papa's German, but I think it is. He never comes along on our visits to Rotterdam.

Now I'm looking out the farm-facing window, still waiting for Opa. At the end of our backyard, the blackberry bushes start and wander off into the countryside in lots of directions. I could swear they get bigger every year. I love to play back there—especially with Johanna. I don't ever remember a time when I didn't have a few scrapes on my arms and legs from the thorns. The farmers in the fields work so hard to raise crops, but blackberry bushes grow all by themselves without any help.

I'm getting impatient, so I enter Opa's study to wait there. In his left second drawer is his drawing kit. Precise instruments to make perfect circles and angles. Papa tells me Opa designed this house with that kit.

Opa lets me play with everything in his desk. Using the compass, I draw a perfect circle. Then I draw myself in it. I've done this so many times. But I'm older in the picture than in real life. And my hair isn't short. But I can't stop drawing circles with slightly different sizes. Once I caught myself drawing dozens of overlapping circles around the picture of me. I'm not smiling in any of these pictures. I think a lot when I'm drawing the circles.

To me, getting older just means harder jobs. Johanna works harder than I do, and I know I'll have to be like her soon. She even makes dinner sometimes. Math problems get harder. Books lose their pictures and are more challenging to read. I learn so much better with Opa, because there's no pressure.

My parents fight about me when they think I'm asleep. Papa was angry with Mutti because she yelled at me about my school grades. Mutti shot back with, "She has to get good grades because she's not pretty." My whole body froze in bed when I heard that. I'm not really sure what grades have to do with being pretty, but it's very bad somehow. I think Papa would like to be more like Opa, but he can't make it happen.

They don't know how good I am at English. I speak it a lot better than they do. I have to keep from laughing when they try. There's an American couple down in the village with a new baby, living in an old, crooked apartment. I heard them speaking English and jumped in to their conversation. They asked me where in America I was from. I fibbed and said, "Seattle."

I think about America a lot. Maybe I could be a different person there.

Johanna's pretty; even I can see that. It makes people, all kinds of people, happy to look at her, and they look at her longer than they mean to. I, on the other hand, make people nervous. Except for Opa, people don't like to look right at me.

And everyone always wants me to do better than I am doing. They say it's because they want the best for me. But it doesn't feel good. The older I get, the further behind I am. I don't have enough friends. I haven't finished enough homework. My room is not clean enough. I wasn't polite enough to my parents' guests. And the hardest of all: people don't like me enough.

It's really hard work to get people to like you. Or maybe I'm especially easy to dislike.

Opa's study has a big mirror on the door. Standing in front of it, I'm surprised by how white my skin is. My hair is black, and I have a big nose. Opa says that's because most of the families in town have Roman heritage, and that I must have ended up with the local hair and nose. Opa tells me this town has been around for at least a hundred generations. We go for walks in the hills around the village, and he shows me where the Roman roads, walls, and vineyards were. How can anyone know so much?

Even better, Opa is the one person who knows *me*. Last week he brought me a present from Bonn. I opened up the long, little box and removed a black, elegant Pelikan fountain pen. It came with a bottle of ink.

He then pulled out a fresh new ledger. I had to laugh. Opa knows how much I hate math at school. It doesn't feel real—like somebody got paid to think up a bunch of problems to drive kids like me crazy. But Opa keeps telling me how important math is for real life, even if I don't think so now.

For the rest of that afternoon, Opa taught me double-entry book-keeping in ink. Real-life stuff I can actually use even now, when I'm nine years old, to keep track of the little money I earn and spend. He told me that reckoning in German marks was only for practice, because they were going to disappear in a few years, replaced by the euro.

He also taught me that money is magic, and that if you give a lot of it away to improve the world, you'll always have more left over than you started with. That's not what my teacher says about subtraction, but I know, without a doubt, that Opa is right, as usual.

He showed me his accounting books, going back to the 1940s. The numbers got bigger and bigger over the years.

"How does that work?" I asked.

He showed me the number in a special column telling how much he gave away last year. I gasped, and my hand came to my mouth. "That's how," he answered.

I asked him what I would do if I made a bookkeeping mistake with the pen.

"You won't," he said and smiled.

Opa believes in God. My parents are not so sure. This confuses me all the time. Opa takes me to church on Sundays. We walk down the hill together. He and I are *evangelisch*—Protestant or Evangelical.

It's hard to translate the term into English. Most of our neighbors in Oberwinter are Catholic. Our stone Protestant church is very small, very old, and musty smelling. The temperature is always cooler inside than outside. I sometimes fall asleep there on Opa's shoulder, and he likes that.

The organist is amazing. She plays on national radio. And the organ is very old: 1722 is painted on the pipes. For the rest of my life, I'm going to make sure I can listen to organ music. My imagination can go almost anywhere when she's playing. After every Sunday service, the organist gives a little concert from the rear balcony where she sits. We stand, lean on the pews behind us, and watch her. We always clap when she's done.

Johanna comes with us sometimes, but Opa says it's important to go to church only when you want to. For whatever reason, Opa and I always want to. Maybe it's just so we can spend Sundays together, but I know Opa would go even if I didn't exist. It seems to help him be happy all the time and everywhere. I hope he'll teach me this magic when I'm old enough.

I don't understand much about what goes on in church, but I love it when they read the Bible stories for children's worship, and the littler kids come and plop right down on my lap, as if they belong there. This Sunday was the story about Joshua and the walls of Jericho. The German Bible says the Israelites were blowing trombones, and Opa's English Bible says trumpets. Things like that make me think.

I hear the door.

Opa's home.

*

1999

Zarzamora, California

Josh

AN HOUR AGO, I RODE MY BIKE up to our home at 119 Mure Street and left it lying there in the front yard. It's not like anyone is going to steal it—everyone knows everyone in our town, and everyone knows that my bike is my bike.

I left in the middle of Little League baseball practice because I got this picture in my mind of an image I had to put on paper. No one saw me sneak out.

I'm so tired of organized sports. I've been on teams since before I can remember. My room is full of trophies I don't care about and didn't put up. My father, Michael, was on the German Olympic basketball team and came to California to try to break into the NBA. He rode the bench for several years, and somehow we ended up here in Zarzamora.

He says we're moving back to Europe someday, where my parents are from, but I don't think that's happening anytime soon. My mom would love it, but we'll see. Dad is pretty important in town and goes to a lot of chamber of commerce and youth sports meetings. He has an insurance office on Water Street (not sure why they call it that—it's really a main street, and there's not a lot of water around).

Northern Europe is freezing cold. I'd rather be outside, and it's harder to do that there. It gets so dark there in the winter that you'd never believe it. My grandparents have a vacation place in Hossegor, France, which is kinda like California, and I'd much rather be there than up North—I love the beach. Mom's folks are rich...at least I think so.

Our own beach is forty-five minutes away—at the end of a winding road that goes downhill through lots of tunnels to Santa Barbara. I think about being there all the time.

Our town looks like it's about to fall apart, but it never quite does. My school looks especially bad. My drawings have a shape to them; our town does not. It looks like everything in it was all put here by accident.

I'm drawing that image from my "vision" at baseball practice as I tell you all this. I draw all the time.

And I love to read. My mom tells me to help myself to her bookshelf. I've read all of the Dutch-language Thea Beckman teen novels. My mom taught me to speak and read Dutch. My dad's German books are for grown-ups and they're too hard, at least for now. But he never speaks English to me at home. So I guess I speak three languages. It's also useful to speak Spanish around town—nobody my age or younger uses it, but a lot of their Mexican parents do.

My dad says my endless hours on a skateboard are a waste of time, but I always think about skating as I'm falling asleep. The parking lot at the abandoned Dairy Queen is my own private skate park.

Mom is really into church. She grew up in Ommoord, Holland, just outside of Rotterdam. Her mom and grandparents live on the top floor of an apartment building when they are in Holland. She talks about her little church there all the time. I've been there, and they meet in a warehouse. They sing with their hands in the air and get a little strange. They all have a certain look in their eyes that I don't fully understand. I always draw designs in my notebook when I sit there with Mom.

We go to an independent nondenominational church in Zarzamora. It meets on Sunday nights in the old Methodist church built in 1906. The Methodists who meet on Sunday morning seem really elderly to me, but they are nice to us.

I keep trying to find ways not to suit up for sports teams, but it hasn't worked. When Dad's not coaching, I can usually skip out, grab my board, and skate somewhere. Dad wants me to learn how to ski, but as you can guess, I just want to snowboard. Dad is so old-school. Our town is the gateway to Gold Mine Ski Resort, uphill a little ways from here. A lot of traffic comes through here on winter weekends. We're used to the musical clanking of chained tires going up and down Water Street.

I hang out with my best friend, Sam, and his dad at their pizza place Friday and Saturday nights. It's against some rules, because we're too young to work, but Sam's dad pays us cash to help out when it's busy. You wouldn't believe how much I've saved up.

I'm tall for my age, like Dad was as a kid, except he's clumsier than I am. There's a big wall behind our neighborhood, and behind that is an abandoned orchard filled with coyotes, blackberry thickets, and rabbits. I've been walking along the top of that stone wall for as long as I can remember. Parts of it are broken down—it's a shortcut to school that no one else my age has the guts to take.

I'm sitting in my room at my drafting table (found it in an abandoned building behind the wall). I draw designs for my skateboards and hope to draw comics someday. Sam has access to his dad's massive collection of late-1960s Marvel Comics editions, and we sit over there for hours, making up stories and characters while we browse through the dry, yellowing pages. I like *Daredevil* best.

When the weather's bad, I can draw for hours. The window on my right looks out on the long wall I walk along on the way to school.

I'm drawing a heart. Not like the one you'd see in a Valentine card. One like an *X-Men* comics artist would draw. First I lay down the light pencil work. Then I go over it with ink. When it's finished, I erase the pencil lines. There are lots of ways to add color if I want to. This heart is edgy looking. Now to finish drawing the image that came to me earlier, when I was at baseball practice...

I had stopped focusing on where I was standing (first base), and a pale girl, who looked familiar somehow, handed me this heart design. It was circled with gnarly blackberry vines with big thorns. She had climbed over the broken wall behind our house to give it to me. She was even thinner than I am.

I thanked her in German. "*Danke.*" An older man I couldn't see, who was behind the wall, called her back after her task was complete.

As I looked down into my hands, I realized that the image was made of iron. A heavy disk with the design on it...

Then the vision disappeared, and I was back at first base, just in time to catch the throw from third.

I'm drawing from memory, even though I've never "seen" this before. My mom says that writers like Thea Beckman do that—they remember a story that hasn't happened and write it down.

Now the drawing is done, and I'm staring at it.

Sometimes when I stare at things my vision goes fuzzy, and I can think really deeply. I'm not sure where I learned to do this, but it feels the same as when I'm snowboarding on the half-pipe at Gold Mine.

Mom often wakes me up from these visions and asks me what I'm thinking about. I never know how to answer. It's a third world. There's also a normal first world we all live in and also the second world of our sleeping dreams. I like world number three best of all— dreaming while you are awake. It's kind of like reading.

I'm always having to hide my designs. If my parents knew how much time I've wasted drawing, they would freak. They think I'm doing homework.

Mom works at the Zarzamora Winery outside of town. She

hosts wine tastings in the summer and winter. No one comes through town much in spring and fall, so she's always at home during those seasons. Mom gets a lot of free wine sample bottles, and I especially like the designs on the labels. I soak them off of the glass and attach them to my drawings. Someday I'm going to design those labels. Even better artwork than the ones I collect now. Ideas come to me while I'm sitting in school.

The ThornHeart design keeps coming back into focus as I sit here at the drafting table.

Picking up a Sharpie, I start to draw a perfect copy of it on my right wrist (I forgot to tell you I'm left-handed and I ride board sports goofy-foot). Dad says they always have use in the majors for left-hand pitchers.

But I don't like sports where we throw, kick, and shoot things. I like to throw and shoot my own body around. Why send something into motion when you can go into motion yourself and enjoy the feeling instead of watching it? I especially like cartwheels. They say boys can't do them, but they are so wrong. I never go a day without cartwheeling. I can even cartwheel along the top of the old stone wall. Mom would wig if she saw that. For an instant in the middle, you feel weightless. There has to be a way to make that moment last longer.

The sounds of the local marching band wake me from my visions. Interesting how the wind direction makes it louder or softer.

Dad watches sports on TV all the time. I like to be with him, so I try it almost every day, but I often fall asleep. TV is like a fourth world. I like the other three worlds better. We're not really a part of the TV world. If we disappeared, it wouldn't even matter to the TV. I've watched my dad while he's watching sports, trying to figure out what's happening in his mind. But I don't get it.

Mom hates it when I draw on myself. I remember, as I look at the ThornHeart on my wrist. But I decide to color it in with red anyway.

Reminds me of the hearts that the statues of Jesus and Mary show us at St. Catherine's Roman Catholic here in Zarzamora. The church is almost never locked, and I sometimes go in there and draw with a clipboard. Jesus and Mary appear to be holding their rib cages open for us to see their hearts.

Mmm, if you took that crown of thorns from the other statue and put it around my heart image, then…

I enjoy the smell of the Catholic church. Nothing else in town has the same scent. A mix of perfume, campfire smoke, wood, and mold. The light coming through the colored windows is amazing as it moves across the wood grains on the pews.

I draw on everything. I draw all over the insides of my school-books. I draw inside the Bible I take to church. I doodle in the margins of my worksheets. I like to erase the eyes of people in magazine pictures and draw in new pinpoint eyes. My mom thinks that's creepy, but I laugh my head off when I look at it.

Church sometimes feels the same as all the team practices. It also feels a little like school. There are rules, groups, and patterns. Every game has rules.

It's like we and the Catholics at St. Catherine's are on different teams. But we don't have enough pictures and stuff to look at as they have. On the other hand, we have great music with a band. Sometimes when we sing, I go to that same place as when I stare at pictures or do cartwheels. I wonder if that happens with the Catholics too. My mom raises her hands in the air and almost dances. Her closed eyelids start to twitch. I love watching that, but I'm not sure why. I think she sees Holland, her home, and her family when that happens.

She misses them and talks about them all the time. Many nights, she pours a glass of local red Cabernet Sauvignon (with a cool label) and writes them a crinkly blue aerogramme in Dutch. I think it's old-fashioned to write letters, but she looks relaxed and happy doing it.

She and Dad would like to have had more kids, but they don't seem to be able to. It would be easier for me if there were more kids in the house. My parents spend too much time thinking about me, and I spend too much time trying to avoid that focus.

I hear them talking about me at night when they think I'm sleeping. The more they say, the more I can tell they don't "get" me at all. They are so stressed, and I'm really not afraid of anything. I've even skateboarded down the crazy-steep Edwards Street hill. No one else has ever made it to the bottom on a board, even to this very day. I started to get that cool "cartwheel" feel when I knew I was going too fast to bail. Like right after you yell "droppin' next!" at the half-pipe at Gold Mine.

I shred. I rip. Whatever you want to call it. I rocketed past a cheering Sam that day on the way down Edwards. Guys were watching from the top and bottom. When I flattened out into a cruise at the bottom, my hands shot up, like Mom's do in church. I was going too fast to hear my own victory shout.

The older kids have called me J-Bro since that day and give me fist-bumps and props when they see me. My parents both call me "Yosh" for short, and it's embarrassing when my friends are around. Their accent can be so cheesy, but I suppose they can't help it.

I really like this ThornHeart design. I'm going to have the guy down at the Asian restaurant make me a Chinese ink stamp of it so I can stamp this design all over the place whenever I use paper for anything. I can also stamp it in the books I read. It would look cool in the Thea Beckman books on the inside covers.

If I leave my room now, I can get out of here before my parents get home. I feel like I get points every time I succeed at fooling them. Who's keeping score, though?

Back on my bike, I look down at the lock chain that holds the paper ThornHeart design down in my bike basket and keeps it from blowing away. I'm the only one of my friends who can ride with no hands. But I do wear a helmet all the time; it just makes sense. Besides, a helmet is another surface on which to draw things. I'm going to spray-paint over the old designs so I can put this new one, the ThornHeart, in the front.

Mr. Park is Korean, and his accent is hard to understand. The restaurant has Chinese and other Asian food. He watches a little TV with Korean shows at the cash register during the day. Like the Catholic church, it smells cool there.

He greets me with a big smile and calls me "Mr. Josh-wa." We work out a deal for twelve bucks for an ink stamp, and he says he'll have it ready for me in a few days. He keeps the picture. It's okay. I memorized it before I ever saw it. He'll include a red ink pad.

Now I'm back on the bike and heading home for supper. It's been a great couple of hours. I can't help but wonder if I'll dream about the pale girl tonight. Hope I can find some more time to draw and dream before I go to bed.

I'll have to steal it from my parents, though, because they would rather I lived in their world.

~ BEHIND THE STORY ~
Angelo

It's dark out, and I'm sitting in another blackberry bush, this one outside of an ancient church in Rotterdam.

Sometimes it's the chance encounters that make all the difference. I'm about to witness one of them. Imagine all of the seemingly random events that lead to your very existence. Change one detail, and you'd never even be here. Do you know your backstory? If not, why not dig a little…discover and experience the mystery for yourself?

Right now the warm summer rain is drenching me, but it feels good.

I've been strolling around a cemetery in Hillegersberg—an upscale suburb of Rotterdam, Holland—killing time, waiting for the big encounter.

I'm on top of a hill, if you can call it that. More of a mound, here in the middle of the cemetery. Holland is pretty flat, so it stands out. And the old, imposing, dirty-brick Protestant town church, with this suburb grown up around it, commands the view from all directions. I have a hunch that people have been meeting on this hill for centuries—perhaps millennia. Maybe it's an ancient burial mound of some kind. The church itself has its own mythic-sounding name: Hillegonda.

To the right is the side entrance to the church through the ornate, open black-iron gate. Bright light from the chandeliers is streaming through the clear church windows into the soggy night.

The Meere organ is leading the congregation in singing the Psalms of Zion. Dutch people are psalm singers by nature. Many of them learn the psalms by heart without even trying, and Psalm 42 is their favorite: "As the hart panteth for the water...."

Over to the left, emerging out of the dark into a streetlamp-lit halo, is Walter, a German. It is the heart of World War II, and Germany is occupying Holland. Rotterdam has been especially hard-hit, and much of the city lies in shambled ruins after the iron fist of the German Luftwaffe bombed Amsterdam's twin town back into the Stone Age.

The summer of 1943
World War II
Hillegersberg, outside Rotterdam
German-occupied Holland

WALTER WALKS TOWARD THE GATE, checking his elite Ziffer à Grande Complication 1924 Swiss watch. It is his special treasure, given to him by his proud father right before Walter left for his military assignment in Rotterdam. His particularly emotionless face seems drawn in by the music and the light from the nearby church.

An officer in the German army, Walter is from an aristocratic Rheinland family that used to do business here at the downstream North Sea port of Rotterdam. Tonight he is off duty and going for a walk in civilian clothing to clear his head. He misses his wife and young son, Harald, back in Germany, and it seems strange for him to be the "enemy" in this city so familiar to him. His father's company has had an office for years, on and off, in this vital seaport.

Walter's father is an elder in the little Protestant church back home in Oberwinter. Deeply patriotic, the Dornbusch family has supplied high-end officers to army after army, war after war. His great-great-grandfather led the premier Prussian division into the pivotal Battle of Sedan. Walter's father was decorated with the Iron Cross. But it isn't likely that Walter will follow in those heroic footsteps. He's stuck here in occupation duty in Holland, in charge of the rebuilding of the Rotterdam infrastructure that his own nation's air force destroyed. Nothing like pouring concrete in the middle of rubble.

The foolishness, futility, and irony of it all have led him out to get some fresh air. His current project, the pedestrian/bicycle/auto tunnel under the river not far from the elegant port terminus of the Holland-Amerika steamship line, is meant to be an Autobahn link in the network of Greater Germany, into which Holland will eventually be absorbed.

His colleagues are readying plans to move half the Dutch population out of Holland to the steppes of partially conquered Russia to homestead new farms side by side with Germans, after the final victory.

Walter is the first in a long line of officers who will have no thrilling battle stories to tell his son. He's authorized to carry a sidearm but doubts he'll ever fire it. He's a bureaucrat in a military uniform.

But Walter's life is about to take a turn he'd never expect.

How pathetic, he thinks as he walks through the gate toward the side door of the church. *Any glory is gone from my life.*

He pauses at the door of the church. *I can pass for civilian Dutch in these clothes*, he thinks, *as long as I don't have to say a lot.*

It has been a long time since Walter has been in church. But the sound of the organ reminds him of his home congregation, and all that home means to him. Homesick and a little depressed, he opens the door and walks in.

Placing his wet umbrella in the stand with the dripping others, he realizes, awkwardly, that he's late for the Sunday evening service and that this door opens near the pulpit. Every eye in the place turns to him briefly as he moves quickly to the left...and out of the line of sight.

There's an empty place on a bench next to an elegant young woman with wavy, shoulder-length dark hair that peeks out from under a brimmed hat. He can't see her face from this angle.

Walter sits down, not sure if he is wet mostly from perspiration (it's a humid summer night) or the rain. But he feels wetter than everyone else in the room. Grief and disappointment well up inside him. Both seem out of place in this ancient holy place that overflows with goodness and promise.

As the sermon winds down, the congregation rises to sing another psalm from their little black books, and Walter shares a book with the young woman he noticed earlier.

As the organ prelude pauses for the congregation to begin singing, something otherworldly happens.

Her voice, clear and potent, resonates with Walter's very body. They say the precise pitch/note that gets produced when you "ping" a crystal glass, when amplified, will shatter the glass.

She's not even looking at the book. This psalm is coming from a deep, deep place—perhaps from the patriarchs and matriarchs of her proud nation.

"*De afgrond roept tot den afgrond* (Deep calleth unto deep)..."

Something like crystal shatters in the back of Walter's throat, and little pieces of emotional broken glass catch in his mouth.

In that very instant, this young woman outranks him, both emotionally and socially. Some people just have power over others. Walter chokes up and struggles for breath. He has to sit down. While she continues to sing forth, a wave of emotion rolls over Walter. All the seeming vanity of his pointless, non-heroic life rolls in hot tears down his cheeks. It is simply impossible to stay dry in any way tonight.

He gathers himself and automatically looks up and to the left. She has placed her perfectly manicured hand on his shoulder. Her concerned brown eyes match her resonant voice. "*Gaat het, meneer* (Are you okay, sir)?"

That face.

How can someone so young—at least ten years his junior—have such an "arrived" countenance? Here he is, the occupying soldier, and his heart defers to her instantly.

In a few minutes, he's regained his composure—taking part in the church service with the rest of them. Walter leaves quickly after the blessing, wondering whether the Dutch black-robed minister would still bless him if he knew he's German.

Rounding the corner into the neighborhood with broad sidewalks and massive leafy trees, he slows down and glances up at the moon that's trying to break through the thickly clouded sky.

Hearing sudden footsteps next to him, Walter pivots, startled.

The woman's eyes look up from under the brim of her hat. "I'm Cornelia. But everyone calls me Nellie. And your name, sir?"

She reaches out her elegant hand to him. Instinctively he bows and kisses it, as if a knight with a princess at court.

"Walter, *Gnädiges Fräulein* (graceful young lady)," he whispers politely after the kiss.

Her other hand shoots to her mouth as she steps back quickly.

A German.

*

11 September 2001
Oberwinter am Rhein, Germany
Just south of Bonn

Opa Harald

OPA HARALD SITS ALONE at the kitchen table in the Dornbusch family home, turning an antique key over and over with his fingers. He has finally located the key to his father Walter's sea chest.

Kati has been begging him for years to open it, but it isn't in Harald's nature to force or break things open. He always waits until the time is right. He likes working with a tailwind, not a headwind.

I promise, Kati, as soon as I find the key, he has always told her.

So now he has found the key. This afternoon they will open the lock and solve the mystery together.

Kati will soon come home from school, and they will have their customary, daily tea-and-debrief session at the kitchen table, looking out over the rolling farm fields to the west and beyond the blackberry thicket defining the boundary between their back garden and the cultivated fields behind the family home.

The Rhine River cuts a deep canyon through this rolling farmland region, and wine grapes are grown on the steep hillsides leading down to the river.

Opa Harald's father, somewhat agitated for whatever reason, had given Harald the key to the chest many years ago and made him swear he wouldn't open it until after Harald's mother passed away. The years passed, and Harald had misplaced the key, probably during the move up the hill into the home Harald had built for the family.

He had been daydreaming yesterday morning at sunrise when a vision came to him....

He was very young in the dream, maybe eighteen. He and a fiery-eyed, fine-featured girl of perhaps ten years of age were sitting on canvas stools in front of a tent. Postcards were floating toward them, originating from behind them. The cards were emerging from a cabin window deep in the woods, then floating in a single-file line through the air on a gentle breath of wind. They would pick them out of the air in front of them and read them together.

Some of the postcards had scenes from California. Some seemed older and had vintage European photos and stamps.

All the messages they pulled out of the floating postcard row were handwritten and addressed to both of them:

You kept your promise. Thank you.
—Your father, Walter

God inside of me loves to dance.
—Janine

You know the girl who is reading these with you, but you've never met her.
—Nellie

It's always the right time to do the right thing.
—Ruud

It must be possible to make cartwheels last forever.
—Joshua

I am so very sorry. So very sorry.
—Nellie

Pay attention to the direction of the river.
—Saahir

*The key to my father's sea chest is in the bottom left
drawer in a small box in my workshop, where I put
it years ago.*

This last one was in Harald's own handwriting.

Funny thing, though. Each postcard vanished into thin air as
soon as the next one was grasped....

The whistle of the teakettle shatters Harald's delicate memory
of yesterday's vision.

Who are Janine, Nellie, Ruud, Joshua, and the others? The
answers will come, Harald knows, as they always do, in time. Kati
will be home shortly.

As Harald waits for the tea to steep, he feels a sense of deep
thankfulness that the visions and dreams are returning.

When Harald was a child, the visions had been as plentiful as
crisp autumn leaves raked up into big piles.

*Can it have something to do with the fact that fall is around the
corner again?* Harald thinks. *The air is already carrying a certain
coolness about it.*

*Why do we lose touch, in the middle of our lives, with visions and
dreams?* Harald muses. *Well, at least they are starting to come back.
Perhaps it is because, in the middle of our lives, we work too hard and
imagine too little.*

He sighs. *Dreams and visions are fragile and subtle things. The
harsh midday sun of anxiety and stress can burn them out entirely.
They need gentle cultivation.*

That's why, Harald is convinced, it has taken him so long to remember where he'd put the key. But today, sure enough, the antique key that he again flips over and over with his fingers on the table was found exactly where the postcard said it would be. Harald is tempted to open it first without Kati, just to take a peek, but he musters all the discipline he can to wait for her. Harald has always been good at patience.

Last evening, when he kissed Kati good night on the forehead, he'd promised: "Tomorrow we open the sea chest together, after school."

Awakened from the memory of last night's tuck-in by Kati's approaching steps, Harald turns toward the front door and takes a mental photo of his granddaughter as she comes through the door and breaks into her only-for-grandfather smile.

She has gotten so very tall, almost as tall as he is. She is still almost painfully lean—a little too nervous in personality to have a good appetite. Having lived through the War himself and all its hardships, it is hard for him to watch her pick at her food and just push it around the plate.

Kati has braces on her teeth, hardly an upgrade on her somewhat homely face, dominated by that nose of hers.

Her skin is as pale as the day she was born, and her hard-to-tame short black hair has broken free of this morning's attempts to groom it.

But to Harald, she is beautiful. She is his beloved granddaughter.

*

Kati

I GLANCE AT MY BIG GLASHÜTTE WRISTWATCH as I approach the front door. I have been waiting all day for the hands of this watch to come to these precise places.

Today we open the sea chest!

Ola, Opa! There's the teapot and the Deventer cake sitting ready on the table. It's the only time of the day I'm actually hungry.

Opa wants our customary teatime first before opening the treasure chest. I'm going to tell him that I feel better inside today. Having something to look forward to makes me feel less agitated. Most days, I'm like a washing machine that never turns off. I can adjust the buttons, water, soap, etc., but there is no on/off switch. I just agitate and agitate....

Mutti is more and more dissatisfied with me every month. Apparently I am not what she had in mind for a daughter. It's not that I won't do what she says. I simply can't. How on earth am I supposed to become beautiful, popular, and good at school? I'm doing the very best I can, and it's not working at all.

Papa is always away in Berlin, and when he comes home, he's very uncomfortable around me. I can tell Mutti has talked him into trying to work on me.

I've started to lie to Mutti. I made up several friends to tell her about that she would like, and they don't even exist. I also pretend to her that I'm popular. But I see people's eyes at school. Very few of them seem glad to see me. When I get nervous, I look at my watch. It's hard to like eye contact when the other eyes aren't looking very warmly at you.

I also run my hands through my hair a lot when I'm agitated. I can't stop doing it. I hate my hair. Mutti still makes me cut it so I can be safe working with Opa's tools. Nothing makes me angrier. I try hard to look like a girl, but I really don't. I despise looking like this.

School is getting harder. Our math teacher draws more and more equations on the whiteboard. To me, it's all a game some person with no sense of humor made up. What's a number anyway? Seriously. Show me one. They aren't real.

Johanna, my big sister, is away on a class trip. She's beautiful, so her life is easy. She doesn't have to play games.

As for me, life is a game I keep losing. "Remember that you are a Dornbusch!" Mutti says to me with her strong Dutch accent almost every week. (She also pronounces *Zinfandel* wine as "ZEENfandel" and drinks way too much of it.)

I have no friends up here on the hill. The girls my age feel like they are ten years older than I am, since they are all good at things that I'm not. Only the village girls down the hill want to play with me, and Mutti hates it when I do. She calls them "common." That sounds wrong somehow. Why would anyone want to rank people all the time?

Opa walked in on me while I was agitating in his study last week. I had taken out his precision compass and had drawn thirty-six perfect circles around a sketch of myself. Each circle was precisely one millimeter bigger than the one inside of it. I can sharpen the lead with sandpaper to make a perfect point.

I had tried about seven times to draw a face that I like but had to erase each one. I had almost rubbed through the paper where my face was supposed to be.

I don't even know what I want my face to look like. Just different. Please, different.

Opa walked up behind me and put his hand on my shoulder. "Kati, always remember this: be an egg and not a bubble. Eggs carry potential of new life. I'll tell you what that means someday, my darling princess."

He always says "darling princess" in English. Almost everything sounds better in any other language besides German. German is so guttural. I like English best. Even better, it's one of the few things I'm good at.

Some days, I wish I *were* a bubble. I could float up, pop, and vanish. Then the agitation would end.

Other days, like today, being different doesn't bother me as much. Not when I have Opa and teatime to look forward to.

I always drink tea with milk, the English way. Opa says that fine china and silver should always be used and not stored. I noticed that he glanced at my priceless Glashütte watch when he said that.

So here I am telling Opa everything about my day. Why don't I have to lie to Opa? He always says, "There's nothing, Kati, that you could do to make me love you less, and nothing you can do to make me love you more. I just love you."

He says that to Johanna too, but she doesn't need to hear it. People already like her, so when Opa says it, it's extra. I, on the other hand, need to hear it over and over.

"Shall we, then? Your mother will be home by suppertime," Opa asks in English.

"But of course, Grandfather," I reply in a perfect Seattle accent.

I'm relieved that Papa is in Berlin, Mutti is at work, and Johanna is on a class trip. That means I can relax and be myself for a couple of hours.

We head up the main staircase to the upper-floor landing. Opa reaches for the rope, which pulls down the ladder to the attic.

For an instant, a shudder runs through me, coming out of nowhere.

"Did you feel that, Opa? It felt the way a big car accident sounds."

Opa stops on the ladder and thanks me for mentioning it. "My promptings are starting to come back," he explains.

I understand. I've heard his stories for years.

"I had a dream or a vision yesterday," he says. "And yes, Kati, come to think of it, I did just feel something. Something terrible has happened and, very sadly, there is nothing we can do about it."

Opa looked down one more time before continuing up into the attic. "Remember, Kati, we are always in the presence of a God who speaks, but that voice is very, very subtle."

Leaving that unnerving experience behind, we climb into the attic. It's illuminated by natural sunbeams of light from four dormer windows, all of which are slightly cracked open on the bottom for ventilation.

I am *finally* tall enough to look out of them now. I used to have to stand on a box. My favorite view is out of the back right one. I can see the Rhine River freight boats plying up and down the river.

But no time for that now. We have a treasure to open.

The attic is full of all kinds of German postwar stuff. It's also where Mutti hangs the clothes to dry.

There it is in the corner: Great-Grandfather Walter's sea chest. It's massive.

The family coat of arms is painted on the middle of the top cover. A heart with a crown of thorns encircling it, same as the shield on the front gate to our front yard. The Gothic script letters for *Dornbusch* adorn the bottom in a semicircle.

My family has a long story in the sea trade. I grew up hearing all about Seattle, Malaysia, Rotterdam, Alaska, Brazil, and lots of other places. But Papa doesn't seem cut out for the business world. He works for the government, which used to be a bike ride down the river in Bonn before the capital moved to Berlin after the Wall came down. He and Mutti have not been happy together since he got transferred to the new capital.

Opa has brought a sturdy flashlight and a bottle of spray lubricant with him up the stairs. He shoots a puff of it into the old, rusty lock. He then reaches for the key in the pocket of his tweed jacket and places it in my hands to try.

After a little persuasion, the lock gives way, and we open its rusty jaws and lay it aside with a thud on the attic floor. Opa flips on the flashlight, and we start to look around inside the chest.

At the very top is an unfolded note addressed to Harald (Opa).

Harald,
Denk an uns mit Nachsicht (Bertold Brecht).
—Papa

Denk an uns mit Nachsicht, which means "When you think about us, be lenient and gentle."

These words seem to stir something in Opa, because his eyes look wet and his breathing gets funny. I'd like to ask him about his reaction, but I'm too impatient. I want to see what's in the treasure chest.

Under the note on top of the contents are rows of now-worthless wood samples from all over the world: teak, Douglas fir, meranti, etc.

From a bag below that, we pull out what seems to be a tattered prisoner's uniform and documents in Russian.

Opa Harald explains. "Kati, as you know, your great-grandfather spent years in forced labor in Russia, with countless other Germans after the War. I remember the day my mother and I met him at his homecoming in the little train station down in the village. I knew him better from pictures than from real life.

"He was properly dressed in a suit and hat. The suit was too big for him; he was very emaciated and thin. He was carrying flowers for Mother. He was a proud man, an officer, and he walked with perfect posture and a bit of a limp. First he gave me a handshake I will never forget. And then he kissed my mother's hand. He looked away after doing that, which seemed odd."

Opa was an only child. Opa's father, Walter, and mother were never able to have more children because of all the terrible things that happened to his father in Russian captivity.

Next to that bag with Russian things lies a beautifully polished, Asian-looking, wooden box. We break the wrapping strap, which apparently made an airtight seal, and lift the lid to reveal shining classic wristwatches, all couched in plush, deep purple/blue felt crevices. Ziffer à Grande Complication 1924. Girard-Perregaux. IWC. Patek Philippe. Audemars Piguet. 8 Jours. Cartier. Universal Genève. Breitling. Zenith. A Lange und Söhne.

Opa pulls out his reading glasses to identify the tiny print on the watch faces. He mouths the names as he goes from timepiece to timepiece. He unhooks the Rolex from his wrist and exchanges it for the Ziffer. He doesn't speak French very often, but a *"Magnifique!"* rolls off his lips in a whisper.

I can't remember a time when I didn't love watches. I feel like we have won the lottery. We lose track of time as we wind them and hold them up to our ears to hear the ticking.

Imagine adding these to the box in Opa's study! Can anyone feel any richer?

We place the Asian watch chest on the floor. It's never going back in the sea locker. Watches are made to be worn, not stored.

Next, a metal case the size of a large lunch box lies shoved below where the Asian box was. It's very heavy. Opa lifts it (he's very strong) and puts it on the floor. The rusty hinges protest as we open it.

Inside, wrapped in thick paper tubes like little silos, are gold Krugerrands. A small fortune. There is a yellowed envelope with a note:

> *Harald,*
> *Für deine Enkelkinder* (for your grandchildren).
> *—Papa*

"Kati," Opa insists, "this is for you and Johanna from my father, but as hard as it is, I want you to put it out of your mind and promise me you'll never tell anyone. Not Johanna. Not your parents. I will take care of it for you and give it to you when the time is right. If something happens to me, you'll know where to find this box, and I know you'll do the right thing with it. Let's put it back and try to forget about it. It's not good for young people to have a lot of money they didn't earn."

He takes one of the Krugerrands and rotates it in his fingers. "Kati," he says, "life is like a coin with two sides—destiny and random chance. The truth is, each side flows out of the other. Quantum stuff. And life spins and spins."

Sometimes Opa says the strangest things, but I trust him. Reluctantly, I restack the surprisingly heavy gold coins into the metal box and hand it back to Opa. *This will be impossible to forget, Opa,* I think. *What you're asking can't be done.*

And then I reach for what I think is the last bag in the bottom right corner.

Another note from Great-grandfather Walter on top:

> *I could never bring myself to throw them away.*

And again, the same Bertold Brecht quote that was on the first letter we found inside the sea chest: "When you think about us, be lenient and gentle."

Two bundles of letters, several hundred in each batch, are neatly tied with string. One is labeled *Nellie*. The other is labeled *Walter*. The dates range from 1944 to 1979. The addresses are unfamiliar post-office boxes in Rotterdam-Hillegersberg, Rotterdam-Ommoord, Oberwinter, and a military address in Russia.

In the middle of the *Nellie* stack I pull out an old black and white portrait of what appears to be a woman in her fifties. She is so elegant, almost royal, that she takes my breath away.

Why can't I look anything like this? I wonder.

Upon closer inspection, I see that the woman (Nellie?) has a curious gap in her right eyebrow and a rather large scar at the base of her left jaw.

Written in sparkly white ink at a 45-degree angle in the bottom right corner of the photograph are the words *Für Immer und Ewig* (for always and eternally).

No names are included. Odd.

Opa Harald's eyes gleam as they meet mine. "We've found these for a reason, Kati. And today is the right day to find them. This should surprise me, but it doesn't. It just completes a story for me that was missing a few chapters. I think we are about to discover that our lives are a little bigger than we thought they were."

But for now, with many unanswered questions, I glance at my Glashütte timepiece and realize Mutti will be home in minutes. Where did all the time go?

Sure enough, Mutti's frantic, panicked voice shouts up from downstairs, evaporating the mysterious gravity of the letters and replacing it with something much more ominous.

"Something terrible has happened in New York. Kati! Papa! Come quickly!"

*

Opa Harald

THE INSTANT HE SEES THE NAME *NELLIE* on the letters, a chill runs up Opa Harald's spine. He remembers the name from the postcard vision and then the words *I am so very sorry....*

Then Harald sees his own name, in cursive fountain-pen-ink letters, on the top letter from Nellie to his father:

> *Pledge to me, Walter, that you will never tell your wife or little Harald about us. I refuse to destroy your family. Maybe after we are both gone and forgotten, Harald and his little brother or sister (I wonder which it will be?) will meet.*

Harald's brow creases. *A sister? I've never had a...*

~ Behind the Story ~
Angelo

Kati, Opa, and Mutti will stare, transfixed, at the television for hours into the night.

It's September 11, 2001.

It will be many years before the world truly regains its balance again.

But in the weeks to come Harald and Kati will make many trips to the attic. They will take their time reading all of the letters out loud to each other, in chronological order. It will be their secret and their adventure into the past.

For Kati, especially, this is a deeply vitalized season in her life. For weeks on end, she always has something, another letter, to look forward to.

As each letter reveals more and more about Nellie's and Walter's lives, this backstory will begin to intrude into the present, connecting the seemingly random encounters in a startling way....

1943

World War II

The Port of Rotterdam

German-occupied Holland

ON A BRILLIANTLY SUNNY DAY, Nellie, in sunglasses, a simple white shirt, and khaki shorts, rides along the great river on her classic brown Gazelle bike. Her shiny, dark hair is so thick the wind doesn't whip it around much. Her heart is pounding, and she's not sure she can survive any kind of conversation. She's hoping no one talks to her. But she has to pull over, stop on the paved bike path, and stand with her hands on the handlebars to try just to breathe.

She and Walter kissed at the North Sea beach in Scheveningen on Saturday.

She is coming off of a broken engagement with Ruud, the grandson of the prewar prime minister. To make it worse, Walter is married and has a son back in Germany.

For the first time she realizes that she may not survive this war. Literally.

The social stigma for dating an occupying German is infinitely brutal, and adultery, which she feels powerless to avoid, is a moral felony. Standing astraddle her bike, shame and fear thunder into her heart.

Adultery, Nellie thinks, *isn't simply wrong because you get caught. It's plain wrong. I am about to, for the first time in my life, do something intentionally evil for which there is no excuse. This is not a mistake—it's deliberate. I am about to betray my nation. And I am about to betray a woman I have never met. She has every right to scratch my eyes out. And their son...*

A double curse. Collaboration with the enemy and home wrecking.

Lost in her thoughts, Nellie lets go of the bike handlebars, and the bike collapses beneath her. She gets tangled in the bike, trying to avoid its falling, and trips awkwardly to the right onto the path, skinning both hands and her right knee.

Freeing herself from the fallen bike, she crawls away from it.

On her hands and knees on the concrete, she bursts into tears. But she has to see Walter. Now.

*

A SHORT WHILE LATER Nellie and Walter stand a few feet apart from each other at a construction site on the river dike. They face slightly away from each other and look out at the water.

Nellie is standing next to her bike and looking left. Her knee is skinned badly. Walter stands in military posture with both hands crossed behind him, looking right. The buttons on his gray dress uniform shine in the summer sun.

Heavy machinery moves tons of wet mud, and men climb up and down on massive concrete forms, tightening the rebar with huge rusty pliers. Walter is clearly in charge, but only over the men. Nellie is making an invitation that will change their lives and could, she believes, end hers. And he will accept.

The industrial noise is such that no one can hear what the couple is saying to each other.

Without daring to face one another, Nellie rides off, back upstream along the river dike.

Walter remains with the men, but his heart has left to go off with her, never to return.

*

1943

World War II

Oberwinter am Rhein, Germany

Just south of Bonn

BACK IN GERMANY, eight-year-old Harald looks down the hill at the village on the same river, hours upstream from what just happened, and a chill goes over his back. *How can that be?* he thinks. *It's high summer.*

He seems to hear words in the wind—some words that he understands (his father's?), and a woman's voice speaking in a strange language.

"*Verabredet* (meeting agreed)!" he thinks he hears his father say with a formal tone. Harald calls out for his father but hears nothing. Only silence.

His heart darkens. Somehow Harald knows this is a bad thing. A very bad thing.

For whatever reason, Harald turns around and runs home to check on his mother....

*

10 September 2001
Zarzamora, California

Josh

IT'S A CLEAR EVENING. I'm staring out my window at the crumbly brick wall that borders the abandoned orchard behind my house when I feel the earth give a little wobble. I don't give it a second thought, though, because the ground never truly stays still along the Pacific Rim—the Ring of Fire. Mini-quakes happen all the time. An understated, subtle, rolling aftershock waves past me as I sit back down at my drafting table.

I'm drawing another stop sign with my T square. So simple. Just need 45-degree angles to make it perfect. How many of these have I drawn over the years? Dozens? Hundreds? And I don't even know why.

My left hand leads the sketching, and I ask myself a silly question. *Are thumbs fingers?* Of course not. We have eight fingers.

Something is wrong this particular Monday evening, and I don't know what. I'm unsettled somehow. Drawing always calms me down.

It's been a coolish, sunny day. On these hinges between the seasons, when the change comes, you know the old weather patterns of the past season are not going to reassert themselves. Change is going to stick. Autumn is on its way.

You can do so many things with an octagon. Sevens and eights are really the same amount, in a way. Dad (and all the Germans) say there are eight days in a week, and they're right because they count both of the bookends of the week—for instance, Monday and Monday—and all the days in between.

My life is simple and balanced here in Zarzamora. But change is in the air. Dad keeps talking about going back home to Europe. A home that's not home to me at all; it's just where my mom's mother, Oma Adri, lives.

My chessboard, as I glance over to my left, has sixty-four squares—eight by eight. My grandmother, Oma Adri, sent it to me last year. It has marble chess pieces.

The only great thing about going back to Europe would be Oma Adri. I always smile when I think about her. She's so intense—more like a high-strung cat than a person—that she wears me out. She's also really short. At twelve, I'm already a lot taller than she is.

The marble chess pieces she gave me have Spaniards, portraying figures from around the year 1600, in Catholic white, and Dutch freedom fighters in Protestant black. The border of the board is in patriotic Dutch orange, and the whole chess set is a continuous reenactment of the Eighty-Years' War, which gave birth to the Holland we all know.

Dad loves to play chess with me, and he's really competitive. We also have a drawer full of German games like Rummikub.

Oma Adri tells me the most important thing in a game is not winning. It's also not about having fun or making sure you are "doing your best." It's *mooi spelen* (playing beautifully).

Dad believes and lives the opposite. For him, it's all about calculation and winning—even if it's winning ugly, with brute force. He yells when he coaches kids' teams. That embarrasses me.

Nothing against Dad's winning focus, but my whole day, every day, is an attempt at *mooi spelen*. I practice smoothness every day. In every step. In every gesture.

For instance, how you look on your skateboard is everything. It ruins the best trick if you feel awkward while doing it, even if you can land it. Here in Cali, we call it *steezy*. It's a combo of stylin' and easy.

Even when I ride my bike, it's not just about getting there fast. It's about how it feels and looks when you ride. Oma Adri so "gets" me when I talk like this. I especially like throwing in carves, when you swoop left and right on your bike as if you're making big bottom turns with your surfboard.

It doesn't matter if there is anyone around or not, I want every motion (and I love motion) to look and feel good. *Steezy. Mooi.*

Life is like a dance…every single move.

They want to get snowboard racing going up at Gold Mine. How dumb. Riding is so *not* about racing. Nothing is about racing.

I hate it when they turn Olympic skating, one of the most graceful things humans can do, into a competition and nine-point-whatever. *Mooi* has nothing to do with judging; it is about *doing.*

Maybe Dad didn't make it in the NBA with his basketball because he never understood all this. I'll try to walk down the hall to breakfast tomorrow as smooth as a panther, without making a sound. Every motion can be *steezy.* I can sneak up on anyone, even on wild animals that live on the other side of the wall. Coyotes live back there, and someday I'm going be able to stalk them without their knowing it. I'm working on it.

While I've been thinking and telling you this, I've drawn all kinds of connections between the points of the octagon. It looks like an umbrella. Or a compass. Or the steering wheel of a ship. The baptismal font at the Catholic church here in town has eight sides.

I look up from my drafting board at the most remarkable thing in my room. A big print of my favorite painting hangs in my room—Vermeer's *Vrouw met Weegschaal.*[*] Oma Adri gave it to me for Christmas last year.

The woman in the pic is so totally *steezy* and balanced. When

---

[*] To view this amazing painting for yourself, search your internet browser for: "Vermeer vrouw met weegschaal" or "Vermeer woman with a balance"

I'm about to go skate my brains out, I look at the picture and listen to funk legends Earth, Wind, and Fire (I "borrowed" the CD from Mom) as loud as my speakers will go, until I feel the balance the woman in the painting is holding in her hands. She's standing alone, just like Oma Adri, who never married and refused to tell her parents how she got pregnant with my mom.

When we first put the framed Vermeer painting up on my wall, Oma Adri and I turned all the lights off and shined my desk lamp onto the reproduction and talked about it for almost an hour. She tells me that Vermeer, also from Delft, Holland, may be related to her father Ruud's family.

The more you look at this painting, the more you see. Do you see the tension in her left hand? I understand that. Maintaining balance.

The old picture behind her on the wall feels like the vibe I get when I'm sitting in the empty Catholic church here in town, drawing.

The light coming in the window is the coolest part of the painting. The woman's face is so beautiful and balanced—not like the pale girl in my dreams, who is always agitated. I believe the blue robe in the painting belongs to Jesus somehow, and I can't stop thinking about the three gold coins.

The woman has turned her back on the past stories (the picture behind her) and is focusing perfectly on the present. She and I totally get the "in the moment" thing.

And she's pregnant. I've never seen my mom pregnant.

Oma Adri says that the light coming into the window is like God's grace. When you enjoy it, it doesn't mean that someone else gets less of it. God is lavish.

It's the best painting there ever was.

Something inside me says I could walk across water if I could balance perfectly. I sometimes practice trying it in my dreams. The woman in the painting has nothing in the balancing scales. She is just "balancing balance." I think that might be the key to everything. If you could balance balance, you could walk on water.

The pale skinny girl has been showing up in my dreams again. Last night she was wobbling across a balance beam in our high school gym. I quietly walked up behind her on the hardwood floor and grabbed her right wrist to steady her. She wasn't startled. She breathed in and found balance. She's like my dad. She doesn't have balance on the inside, so it's hard for her body to balance on the outside. Some people are falling over inside, 24/7.

I grab my ThornHeart ink stamp and push it down hard into the squishy red ink pad and "sign" my octagon. Too sleepy to draw anymore...

I awake...I think...to a nightmare.

Are Mom and Dad okay?

The ground is shaking back and forth. Glass is breaking.

Everyone is losing balance.

Are Mom and Dad okay?

I'm not just misplacing balance. I'm losing it. My childhood is slipping out of my grip. I am being pulled out of my room into the dark night sky, high above Zarzamora.

There's a sudden scene change in the dream.

I get transposed in the nightmare. I find myself out surfing in the Santa Barbara lineup at night. A rogue wave the size of a sideways semitruck starts to jack up. I desperately try to paddle and claw up the face to top the crest. No go.

I fall backward, the only true sensation of zero gravity on this earth, and the wave crashes down on me.

In the turbulence, I am drawn deep underwater by the leash

attached to my ankle and surfboard. I claw upward toward the blurry light but am pulled downward.

My leash breaks, and I get rag-dolled in the turbulence. The board is my flotation device, and it is gone.

Another twelve-foot wave hits, and the vicious turbulence is repeated before I am able to get a lungful of air between poundings.

But this time the water is hot and smoky. In dreams, some things make sense that don't make sense in the real world.

All of a sudden I find myself facedown on a carpeted office suite floor that is quaking and heaving. I hold my balance. The roar of what sounds and feels like the concussion of an extended train wreck continues to make laps around my ears. I look up and see, through the strangling smoke, broken window glass and sky off to the side.

I run for the opening as the floor heaves and snaps.

Leaping through the broken window into what turns out to be midair, I grasp for any kind of hold, which isn't there.

Looking down, I see an urban landscape one hundred floors below my flailing feet....

Screaming, I sit straight up in bed.

Are Mom and Dad okay?

The ROTTERDAM SPARTA soccer shirt I'm sleeping in is soaked. I have to pull it off....

At last the nightmares evaporate, and morning comes.

I'm standing in the living room with my school book bag and my skateboard, staring at the TV news. The World Trade Center towers are crumbling over and over in rerun after rerun.

Dad peered up into the sky when he went out the front door to meet with the community leaders to assess risk to the town of Zarzamora. He looked worried.

Mom left for work at the winery a few minutes ago.

Waves of what Mom calls "vertigo" keep rolling over me. She told me not to walk to school along the top of the wall, just for today.

It will take every one of us a decade, at least, to get our balance back. If we ever do. Once the season changes, the old one doesn't come back for a long time.

I immediately think of Oma Adri. She would know what to do.

The instant I think of her, the phone rings.

Sure enough, it's Oma.

PART TWO

2001
9-11 Attack Day
Zarzamora, California

Janine

JANINE, JOSH'S MOTHER, STANDS ALONE behind the counter of the wine-tasting room of the Zarzamora Winery.

The radio is on, and Janine has been staring for hours at the polished wood floors as she listens to every word of the news. Now she glances at her exotic Asian ring, and memories start to trigger.

For the first time ever, on a beautiful sunny September day, not one visitor has come in all day. The slow season doesn't usually start until later in the month. She will lock up tonight without having talked to a single person. Even the phone has not rung.

Janine could use the money, so she stays on for the full shift and punches the clock. Having grown up in a prominent, wealthy family, this is quite an adjustment.

She has plenty of time to think about the 9-11 terror atrocities being broadcast through speakers into the wine-tasting room.

Atrocities. Her mind flips to an earlier time—her sixteenth birthday in Holland—when Oma Nellie had taken her to a fancy restaurant at De Bijenkorf Department Store. There Oma Nellie had told her everything that had happened in 1944....

*

1944

Hillegersberg, Holland

ZWANGER (PREGNANT)?

Nellie's mother admits, in the kitchen over afternoon tea, that she suspected as much. Nellie has found it impossible to hide the growing baby, and her mother calls her in to talk about it. Nellie had been playing from Chopin's preludes on the Bösendorfer piano in the solarium.

"*Ja, moeder* (yes, Mother), it's true. And I love the father. Even though he's not in the room, I was playing that for him. He adores my music."

Mother covers Nellie's hands lovingly on the table. "We'll make this right somehow. These things happen, even in our circles."

"Mother?"

"Yes."

"The father is German."

*

AS NELLIE STANDS ON THE STREET in front of Ruud's magnificent home, a few blocks from her own, her mother's words play over and over in her mind: "*Don't ever come home again.*" She can still feel the bruise burning around her left ear caused by her mother striking her after learning the baby's father was German. Her lunge at Nellie knocked the table on its side and smashed much of the priceless tea service.

So, Nellie thinks, *I'm pregnant and showing it, on the street and in wartime, carrying the unborn child of a married enemy soldier. And I'm at the door of the young man with whom I broke our marriage engagement because I knew I didn't really love him.*

She exhales slowly through pursed lips.

Just a few months prior, Nellie had risked what was left of her reputation to accompany Walter, in public, to Rotterdam's Centraal Station, as he was shipped out on a troop train to the Russian front. Every last German soldier was needed to defend the Fatherland as the juggernaut Soviet Army was thundering across the steppes, aiming at Berlin.

As the train started to pull away, Walter silently handed Nellie his magnificent Swiss Ziffer watch through the cabin window. Nellie reached up while running along with the train, grabbed it, and held it to one cheek as she waved with her free hand. She vowed to keep it running until she saw Walter again—the ticking reminding her of his presence and the hope that he was surviving the Russian onslaught.

Not long afterward, she wrote him about the pregnancy. When she didn't hear back, she had no idea if he was even alive. But while writing him, she looked down at the huge man's watch on the desk and noted it was still ticking. So she could at least hope....

Now, as she gazes at Ruud's house, she holds a small suitcase in one hand and her pregnant belly in the other.

*

FROM AN UPPER-FLOOR BAY WINDOW, a wealthy older woman gazes at Nellie. The room behind her is filled with full-length oil portraits of important-looking people wearing orange sashes.

Nellie looks down at her suitcase and up at the house about three times. It takes the older woman awhile to "read" the situation. But when she figures it out, a flood of compassion fills her, and she turns and runs down the stairs.

Flinging open the door, the older woman hurries to Nellie and throws her arms around the girl, lifting her off the ground.

At first, Nellie is startled. The suitcase goes flying and bounces twice. But then her arms return the hug. Oh, how she has always loved Ruud's mother. Family friends, they are. Nellie has grown up calling her Tante (Aunt) Riek.

Nellie inhales the older woman's expensive perfume scent as they embrace on this brisk spring morning.

For the first time, Nellie believes that she and the baby might just live through this war.

Thank you, God. Thank you, God.

~ BEHIND THE STORY ~
Angelo

2003
Melrose District
Los Angeles, California

Kati is pedaling on her beach-cruiser bike past the trendy shops along Melrose Avenue on her way home.

If you can call it home.

She's gotten taller but is still almost painfully thin and pale. Her prominent nose seems to stick out from an unruly, dark mop of hair. Her eyes are hidden.

Kati and Josh have traded continents recently.

In fact they were both in the air, flying in opposite directions, on the same "moving" day: Kati westbound on Lufthansa Flight 119, Frankfurt/LA; Josh eastbound on KLM Flight 911, LA/Amsterdam.

It's typical California "June gloom" weather. Overcast. A hoodie sweatshirt kind of day...

Kati

I DO NOT WANT TO GO HOME.

I love home and hate it—at the same time.

It's always great to walk in and see Opa, who's lived with us since we moved to Los Angeles. But Mutti told me not to come home unless I get a haircut, and I'm not getting one. She used to say it was because she was afraid of long hair getting caught in the power tools that Opa and I would use, but we left those behind with the family that's renting our house back in Germany.

Nowadays, she just tells me it's because I don't have nice hair, and the less of it I have, the better. Well, I'm not cutting it today, and I'm *never* cutting it. It's the one thing I can control about my looks. There's always one pancake in a batch that is shaped funny and a little burned. That would be me.

Johanna's hair is perfect. She's perfect. Being around her—and everybody who makes such a big deal over her—is hard for me. So I stay away from home as much as I can.

Mutti told me that moving to California would be a chance for me to start over, to be more popular than I was in Germany. She meant well, but it made me dread the pressure of coming here and having to perform better, socially, for her.

I still have very few friends, and Americans name everyone their friends. If I were to stop calling or greeting people, I would fall off of the map. No one ever takes the initiative to get to know me. No one, except Zara, really even knows I'm from another country. My

English is perfect, and no one seems interested enough to ask where I come from.

Zara is from Pakistan. There are a lot of Pakistanis and Orthodox Jews here in the Melrose District.

I love the colorful shops here along Melrose. Wish I had lived here all my life. There is so much to see here—so much going on. LA is always in present tense. No one cares about history. It's all about the here and now. So much right-now that it makes you dizzy. I think I just said "so much" three times.

I go in and out of most of the shops on a regular basis. The fashions are way ahead of what we were wearing in Germany. I tell Mutti I'm with friends, but I'm usually shopping alone. Every time I ride all the way through the Melrose District, a storefront has changed hands. There's always something new to look at.

I wish I could resent Johanna for being the always-favored one, but she's so likeable. Should I feel bad for wanting with all my might to dislike her? Why can't *I* be likeable? She doesn't seem to have to work at it. But the more I work at being liked, the worse it works. It's *so* not fair.

And all the girls at school, including Zara, are developing a figure. Not me. Mutti even took me to the doctor to ask what's wrong. I have never been more humiliated in all my life than sitting there in the doctor's office. They can't find anything physical that might be causing it. I just look like a skinny, awkward boy with a lot of hair. I hate walking by mirrors. That's why I never wear jeans or pants—always a stylish skirt or dress. I am traumatized by the thought of people wondering what gender I am. Can you imagine how embarrassing that is for me? Maybe they don't wonder at all, but I worry about it anyway.

There are days when I physically feel like I'm always about to lose my balance. It's hard to describe. It's like chronic tripping... constantly being "off."

I'm afraid of mistakes, so I speak softly and then people always have to ask me to repeat myself—which makes the awkwardness worse.

Mutti bought me new jeans for Christmas last year, and they still have the tags on them. Like I'm going to wear them and have everyone think I'm a boy. Not going to happen. Makeup doesn't work very well, either. My hair is bushy, my eyes are small, my nose is huge, so why draw attention to my face with cosmetics? I'm developing a mega-collection of big sunglasses. No one will have to see my eyes.

And I'm too tall. Way too tall. It would be embarrassing to dance with a boy my age...although I would love to be asked.

Mutti denies she does this, but I believe she works hard behind the scenes to get me invited to parties and beach bonfires. The kids are so friendly here, way more open and sunny than my classmates in Germany. But I don't know how to act around them. I think I could easily tell if a boy was ever interested in me—but that just doesn't happen.

I tell Mutti that the parties go well, because she gives me a social coaching session if I don't. But that encourages her to get me invited even more often. It's a vicious circle. I want to go to the parties, really I do, but I'm also relieved when the plans sometimes fall through. I often leave early, when I can't stand the awkwardness of being around people for even one more minute.

Checking the watch on my skinny wrist (I rotate using about twelve of my favorite classic timepieces from the sea chest, and today it's the Patek Philippe), I see I'm already fifteen minutes late for supper. I'll just tell Mutti that a classmate and I got carried away shopping. I'll have to make up a name. I hate that. I'm running out of names for imaginary friends.

Wearing these watches is like taking Opa with me during the day. He's having a lot of trouble with his eyes and listens to music for hours a day. Funny...I guess. The one person who likes how I look, and now he can't see me very well. He's had two eye surgeries, but I think the doctors are merely guessing about what to do for his vision. We went to the best eye doctors in the world at UCLA, but even that isn't helping.

Opa and I take the Wilshire bus together down to Santa Monica several times a month. I describe things to him en route. While walking the 3rd Street Promenade and the Pier, I put my arm in his and guide him—in such a way that no one else would ever guess he has eye problems. (He has a lot of trouble with curbs.) A couple of my classmates have seen us walking arm in arm. Those are a few of the times since we moved here that I feel truly happy. They saw me with someone who loves me. I blush—but in a good way that feels wonderful.

Opa and I can talk for hours about the secrets we found in the attic back home in Germany. I continue to think about how I am a product of those dramas from generations past.

Papa looks more nervous than ever. The move here to the Los Angeles German Consulate was supposed to be a promotion. I suppose it was, but it seems like too much responsibility for him. Is it wrong not to want to be much like either of your parents?

I've noticed that my parents drink more than anyone else here. Is it just because they're Germans—or because they're unhappy with the way life turned out for them? I'm not sure, but I sure don't want to grow up to be like them. Mutti often has a Bloody Mary first thing in the morning. And Papa is drinking way more than he used to. He still seems so self-conscious around me. We've never had a truly smooth conversation. It always feels a little embarrassing, even when we're not talking about embarrassing things. I don't think it's me. He just has an even more agitated temperament than I do.

I know about their drinking volume, because I raid their liquor cabinet at night when I can't sleep and during the evenings when they're out. I've sampled almost everything they have there—adding water here and there to the bottles. Sometimes I wake up with a throbbing headache, but they haven't caught me yet. They have so many extra bottles that I occasionally sell one to my friends (who are too young to buy it at a liquor store) for extra shopping money.

Californian students are friendly enough. They talk to me when I sit with them, and they seem welcoming. But they never come and sit with me. They only come looking for me if they want access to alcohol. I sometimes pretend I'm low on supply just to keep them coming back more than once so they'll talk to me.

In the middle of the night, with a stolen drink, I often look through the photos of our life in Germany. I miss Opa's shed the most, and the tools. I'm going to start working on movie and TV sets as soon as I'm old enough. I can't wait to work a band saw again. When I'm working with tools, and the fresh sawdust billows up from the sander, my sense of balance comes back and my agitation calms down. I ride my bike past the studios all the time. They're getting used to me, and the security people have started letting me in. I live for those days, and when I'm there, surrounded by the folks making sets, I don't feel off balance anymore. Even though I'm a kid, they even let me help sometimes. I could live on that high for days.

It's a whole 'nother world. I especially love the Paramount lot. They shot *Star Trek* and *I Love Lucy* at these studios, and I'm more at home there than anywhere else, except maybe for church with Opa. Mutti asks me if I'm going to try out for a part some day. She so doesn't get me. I want to build sets and backdrops. If I can't be beautiful, at least I can create beautiful images. Opa merely smiles and states again that I have a superior gift of craftsmanship and an eye for detail. I get excited when I think about doing things like that.

When they are entertaining at home, and diplomats do that a lot, Mutti always introduces me as a "future actress, if she would just cut her hair." She's said it like a bazillion times. Why do parents pick one phrase that bugs their kids and say it over and over to their friends? And besides, my hair's not that long. It's only been over a year since I refused to cut it short anymore.

I've been rehearsing imaginary dialogues all day, trying to figure out how I'm going to react when Mutti turns livid because my hair is not cut. I rehearse these pretend conversations all the time with people who make me nervous. It makes it hard for me to sleep sometimes. That's when I drink. And when I drink, my imagination runs wild. But usually drinking makes me feel worse…darker on the inside somehow.

Wait till the folks at the Paramount lot see what I can do with my hands. They said that in a year or so, maybe, if I'm still interested, I could work a few hours there. Interested? Are they kidding? I'd love that job. And then I'd get to be around people who notice me… and maybe even like me.

Opa says I shouldn't worry about it, but I do. He says we are all worth the same, no matter what anyone thinks. He says the awful war he saw as a child was caused by people who didn't believe this simple truth.

Our school, Bancroft Middle School, is always in mural-painting competitions with other schools throughout LA. That's where I met Zara, my Pakistani friend. She missed our last project. Happens a lot. She's always expected to be there for every family event—no matter what. Opa loves to ask her about her family and sometimes attends the events at her home with me. He and Zara's father seem to have a lot to talk about. "Old school" stuff, I guess.

Our art class had to spend the first hour clearing the wild blackberry bush from the face of the concrete beneath the overpass where we painted the mural that day. I cut the back of my right wrist on one of the thorns. The long, thin scab is still there, and it stings occasionally. I got back at the vine by painting sharp, menacing blackberry vines winding through the mural. But I suppose the plant will grow back and outlive the mural....

Opa kisses me on the forehead every day before I leave for school on my bike. Even as he's gotten older, he always stands up whenever I enter the room. He holds my head in both hands, tells me in English that I'm his darling princess, and then seals it with the kiss where he tells me the tiara should be.

He also says I have a perfect smile, and I should smile more. He calls it my "high beams." At night I practice smiling, because I know he's right. Someday it will come in handy.

Opa and I go to Hope Lutheran Church on Melrose every Sunday morning. I'm mentioning that because I'm riding by it now on my bike—almost home. Papa drives us there on Sundays and picks us up but never comes in with us.

He's missing the best part of the week, as far as I'm concerned. I love my Sunday school class, because I get to help out with the little kids. There's nothing like feeling the arms of a happy two-year-old flung around your neck, or getting kissed on the cheek by a four-year-old who's just eaten a graham cracker. It doesn't get any better than that. I wish everybody was like them…loving with no strings. If I could pick anybody to be like and to hang out with when I grow up, it would be those little kids.

When it's time for worship, lots of studio musicians volunteer to lead worship, and the gospel soloist who leads the service (it's like an amazing concert in which you participate) is spellbinding. She sings out of a place inside her that isn't awkward. Opa says that's called having "soul." Someday I'm going to find that place inside me.

When she sings, my breathing changes and I sometimes have to wipe my eyes. That's when Opa, who always notices such things, pulls me closer with his arm that's often around my shoulder when we sit together.

When this happened last week, he whispered into my ear, "She is so beautiful. Like you."

The simple, modern, white room with a very high ceiling is so different than church back in Germany. At Hope Lutheran we sit in a semicircle, 150 of us, in chairs. Zara might come with us sometime, but she would have to keep it a secret from her Muslim parents. Opa says there are fun adventure secrets and bad secrets. I'm not sure what he means by that.

Zara's home smells like curry. She says ours smells like butter. I'm sometimes so afraid to use the word *friend* out loud with her, because that might ruin everything. When something goes well for me, I start wondering when it's going to unravel. Her mom doesn't speak English at all. She points at me and talks really loud and fast to Zara in Urdu. It makes me feel even more nervous than I usually am. I have no clue what would make her mom happy.

This past Saturday, Zara and I were riding our bikes past all the Orthodox Jews strung out along the sidewalks heading back from synagogues. I'm not sure what "an American" really is, but it sometimes feels like none of them have homes in our neighborhood. Everyone here in the Melrose District seems to have a foot in another country. Zara lives around the corner from our house with her big brother and parents. The family owns a gas station east of our district near the Hollywood Freeway.

There's our white house up ahead on the right. Stucco. The tops of the outside walls have fake castle turrets. The driveway on the narrow lot goes up the left side of the home, along the fence, and into the back by the garage and the back porch where I always put my bike.

~ Behind the Story ~
Angelo

Kati walks through the open back door into the kitchen. There are raised voices.

More raised voices.

A slap.

Kati bursts back out the door, sobbing uncontrollably. She fumbles with her bike—it takes two tries to get her kickstand up—and races down the driveway, making a hard right turn on the sidewalk toward Zara's house.

She won't return home until late tonight.

*

KATI ISN'T THE ONLY ONE who's dealing with some issues. Her friend Zara has more than her share—even ones Kati doesn't know about...at least not yet. Right now Zara is writing in her journal, stopping every now and then to chew on the cap of her pen. I can't help it. I peek over her shoulder. ...

*

Zara's Diary

DEAR DIARY,

This year I made my first real American friend. Well, she's actually German, but whatever.

Her name is Kati.

I've been here since I was a little girl, and she just got here, but she looks more American than I do, and that gives her advantages I don't have.

She's kind of funny looking and wears big men's watches. Her hair is a mess. But I really like her. We both love painting and complaining about our clueless parents.

I'm not a U.S. citizen, since I wasn't born here. But I'm not Pakistani either, because I've never even been back there since I moved here when I was two. In fact, I have no memory of Pakistan at all. And my Urdu is awful. I usually answer my parents in English. Being Muslim has been so hard for my parents since 9-11.

My cousin Saahir is the smartest one in the family, and he says we're going to be fine and that peaceful and generous people always prevail in history. Our parents are trying to get a chain of convenience stores going. Saahir was born a grown-up. They already are starting to ask him what they should do. His English is perfect, and he understands computers and money. He goes to the library to read the newest issues of *The Economist*. What a nerd.

Anyway, Kati and I were painting a mural on an underpass a few months ago with the school group, and we started laughing about our parents. But then she got sad after impersonating and making fun of her mom's Dutch accent.

She took me home to meet her grandfather, who kissed Kati on the forehead when she came home. He seemed genuinely interested in me. Some of the older men in my family don't think girls are worth talking to about important things. My brother gets all the attention in our family. Some of my male cousins get rough with me.

My parents argue about whether they should arrange a marriage for me. That's exciting and scary at the same time. Saahir will be able to marry anyone he wants—by that time he will be in charge of the whole extended family.

Kati's mom came home later on my first day at their house and gave me that look people give Muslims. It's hard to describe. But it makes me feel like a bug.

We've started hanging out together. Kati's and my favorite place to eat is the Blu Jam Café on Melrose, where we split the warm mushroom salad with gorgonzola cheese and spicy pesto. Having parent trouble gives us so much in common. I am also interested in what she and her grandfather do at church. Kati loves to talk about the music there and the kids she teaches.

Kati walked me to my home after that first mural-painting day— we live kinda on the same block—and we talked for hours. We both realized we have it harder than most girls, and we understand being from somewhere else with stories no one here knows about. What I love most is hearing her tell about the Walter and Nellie love story.

In our driveway, she said she had only made-up friends (not sure what that means) and would like to be friends with me. She seemed nervous asking.

Not sure why, but that made me so happy. Kati "gets" me. In any case, we both love to paint.

*

INTERESTING HOW TWO PEOPLE can see their own—and each other's—worlds as so different and so infinitely more intriguing and significant, isn't it?

1944
Rotterdam City Hall
Holland

"HOW CAN YOU BE SO GOOD TO ME?" Nellie asks Ruud as they sit on the steps of the massive city hall. She's in a spring dress and wearing her signature sunglasses and heavy makeup to hide the bruise from her mother. He's in his best gray prewar suit, a little big on him now. Everyone has lost so much weight during the War.

They have just gotten married in a small civil ceremony. No reason to call attention to their questionable situation.

Nellie and Ruud have known each other all their lives. Before the War, this kind of glorious too-warm-for-spring day would have been perfect for ice cream, which they've shared together many times as children. It's been so long, they can hardly even *remember* what ice cream tastes like.

Just yesterday Nellie had shown up, homeless, at Ruud's door. Tomorrow they will leave on bikes for Ruud's family's country villa, which produces enough fruit and vegetables to keep them alive and to give the baby a fighting chance at development. They hope their threadbare bike tires hold up. There are no replacements to be found. Anywhere.

Enjoying their last day in the city before leaving, Ruud looks into the cloudless blue sky and says, without looking at her, "Nellie, I don't care what it took to bring you back to me. This is the best day of my life and an answer to prayer. I don't hold it against you for having left me. I know you aren't in love with me, but I'll love you forever, even if you never see me as 'the one.' For me, you've always been the one.

"I'm going to give your baby a home and take care of both of you. In time, this war will be over, the Germans will be gone, and people will forget. Our family will protect you. You are one of us now."

And then he gathers her closely in his arms.

Ruud had no idea that day just how powerless he really was, nor how powerless he would be in the future. A betrayal far greater than he could ever control was on its way....

But, for now, fast-forward sixty-two years, to the Atlantic Coast of France, for a different kind of betrayal, and an encounter that would send Josh on a trajectory he couldn't plan.

Summer 2006
Hossegor
Atlantic Coast of France

Josh

TODAY I AM FLIRTING WITH BETRAYAL. Not sure I want to tell you about it, but I will. Have you ever thought about the fact that you can't betray a stranger?

I'm looking out at first light in the morning, well before sunrise, from our family's summer-home deck, toward *La Graviere,* one of the heaviest ocean waves in Europe. It's a beachbreak, and I scan every contour of its familiar menacing curl with Oma Adri's binoculars. The swell comes out of deep, deep water and really carries massive freight.

The eight-sided, top-floor cupola room of the house is behind the deck where I am standing. In the center of that room is one of Great-Grandmother Nellie's pianos. She always said that musical octaves and such rooms matched perfectly. I feel like Nellie, though long dead, is watching me from her piano as I'm scanning the waves. I check twice to ensure that the piano bench is indeed empty.

Turning back around to scan the beach, I see overhead to deadly double-overhead waves; that'll keep the tourists away. Water about 71 Fahrenheit/22 Celsius. I could trunk it if the sun were out, but I'll go with my spring wet suit, since it's still early and cool.

Today should be good, I think to myself as I take another sip of dark roast coffee and a bite of my croissant. Look at those glassy wave faces! I wonder if Max will show up in the wave lineup today. Is there such a thing as having pre-regret? Are we best friends or bitter rivals? Maybe both. Maybe neither.

Max.

How do guys get to be friends? It sort of…well, happens. At a certain point, you just realize you are doing a lot together. He lives a couple blocks over in this exclusive enclave, and, having met at family events years ago, we've started ruling the local wave together. But as much time as we spend hanging out, I still feel off balance around him. Somehow I lose my usual crystal-clear focus.

This is my fourth full summer here at the family place, which my great-grandparents Ruud and Nellie built after the War, although I've been popping in now and then since I was very young. The living room is still full of pictures of them with their local French friends from the neighborhood. Adri still hangs out with all of them when she's here. Her mother, Nellie, dominates each yellowing photograph with her regal presence.

Our residential beach neighborhood north of central (the "Ville") Hossegor is almost American-suburban-resort-looking; this is hardly Old Europe. Ruud isn't up to making the trip anymore, so he stays home in Ommoord, and Oma Adri is in charge here until fall. My parents come in and out. I get to stay. I feel totally at home in the neighborhood but am uneasy with the people. Or perhaps, more accurately, they are uneasy with me. Ironically, since I reject my father's attempts to get me into competitive old-school sports, I end up putting a darkish competitive edge on my surfing, which I occasionally hone to razor-sharpness. Somehow *mooi spelen* and *steezy* have turned into an ambient anger that turns people off.

I hurry quietly down the outdoor iron spiral staircase and check out my quiver of surfboards. I'm going with the big-wave "gun" this morning, so I slip into my short-sleeved wet suit and try to flatten my pillow-crazed hair with my hands. A little sticky wax to bump up the surfboard deck, and off I go, barefoot, down the short street, out of the neighborhood, to the crosswalk on the two-lane coast highway.

When I get there, some cars with empty surf-racks are already parked in the sand. I jog up the path to the break. The crash of the wave sounds like a compound cannon shot about every ten seconds. The tide is pushing in, I notice, which will jack it up even higher over the next hour.

It's going to be epic.

Is there enough light to see if Max is in the lineup?

I'm slightly hungover from last night. Hit the Bermuda Triangle of Dick's Sand Bar, Club 15, and Rock Food. Hoping to get sponsored soon so I don't run out of money. Maybe if I win a surf contest?

I'm not just hungover but worn out from all the dreaming last night. Ever since my 9-11 dream, I've been crafting a whole inner world through what Oma Adri calls "lucid dreaming." Much like surfing, it's all about being in the moment when you're dreaming and steering it in a certain direction.

Oma told me that, in dreams, always imagine you are wearing a digital watch and look in mirrors a lot. Mirror images in dreams are never clear. And digital watches don't keep linear time. That way you can tell when you are dreaming.

Lucid dreaming is "dreaming, but knowing that you are dreaming." The pale, skinny girl continues to show up in my dreams. She's always on a beach-cruiser bike and now sometimes wears her hair in a braid. If she's not real, why does she age as I do? Oma showed me in the Bible that dreams often contain messages from God.

I could use a message from God right now. I'm finding it impossible to navigate all the expectations from my father, my friends, myself, and even God. It's all one ball of wax. And it's suffocating.

Life seems to be a no-win game, even if you play it especially well. We're forced to bargain for deals that contradict other deals we've already made. And resigning from the game ends up being only one more move—and a bad one—in the same game you just tried to leave. So I'm searching for answers.

When we're in Hossegor, Oma and I go to the Eglise Nouvelle Vie—a little storefront church with mostly African French-speaking members. Many of the immigrants at Nouvelle Vie work in the tourist industry.

Needless to say, they must have been surprised to see an aristocratic Dutch woman show up for the first time, years ago. Doubtless, she has more money than any of them, and it wouldn't surprise me if she ensures the pastor's salary and makes sure the rent is paid. They've nicknamed her *Le Feu*—The Fire.

She often goes for long walks by herself after church. My guess is that she wants to talk out loud to God and doesn't want anyone to hear it. She once asked me why I thought that the Bible is full of genealogies, and she and I both knew, during that discussion, that there was a torch of faith that someday would be passed from her to me. There are family curses—but there are also family blessings and carriers of the flame.

Once the Senegalese church members prayed over me at the end of the service, and I blacked out and fell back onto the floor. I spent what felt like days in a vision—walking along the top of an endless broken stone wall back in Zarzamora. The blackberry bushes had grown to ridiculous heights on both sides and began scraping and gouging my bare arms as I tried to walk on. At a certain point, I was absolutely trapped by the vines, panicked, and then woke up on the carpet of the church. Asking how long I was out, they replied, "About three minutes."

My three worlds—reality, dreams, and my ideal vision/ inspiration—flow in and out of each other all the time. Whenever I have a foundational dream or vision, I stamp my calendar in red ink with the Asian ThornHeart stamp I had Mr. Park make for me back in Zarzamora. There are more and more marks every month.

Mom and Dad, or should I say Dad, is struggling since moving back to Europe from Zarzamora. Dutch kids would rather play soccer or basketball at a playground *without* adult supervision than be in some youth league, so there is very little opportunity for him to coach. Great-Grandfather Ruud has given him every social advantage, but, although born and raised in Germany, Dad's like a fish out of water over here in the Old World.

I'm embarrassed for him; he's in and out of the generous Dutch welfare system. He's started smoking again (rolls his own cigarettes) and spends hours and hours watching sports on TV. He's getting really opinionated. He puts impossible athletic achievement demands on me, which is ironic, because he doesn't do much of anything himself. It's very clear he wants me to be a more successful version of himself. I don't want to be any version of him. You don't want to count the empty beer cans around his chair.

In a nutshell, he wants me to do team sports as he did, and to score higher. I sometimes worry that my whole lifestyle is a reaction against this expectation rather than something flowing out of my true self. I'm losing my integrity, but so slowly that you can't see it happen.

I always hide my surfboards when he visits us in Hossegor, ever since he took a hammer to one of them in the middle of the night a couple years ago, after drinking for hours. If it wasn't for tiny Oma Adri, with her formidable authority, ordering him back to bed, he would have destroyed my whole quiver of boards.

Mom is spending more and more time at the little warehouse church back near our four-generation penthouse home in Ommoord, Holland, and helps lead singing. I walk there with her most Sundays, down Braambes Street, especially if it's raining and I can't skate. Christian music has always been a path to God for me. I often amp up listening to D.O.C. before I skate.

Oma Adri says honoring your parents isn't as easy as it appears, but she's confident I'll find a way to do it. Is it being super compliant? Then we would end up aligning with their brokenness as well as their gifting. She asks great questions. She once asked: "Do you think Jesus was sinless because he was a compliance athlete?"

I am still "gardening" an answer to that one. It could take time.

It's pretty hard to be at home watching my dad, so I just kick it at the skate park in Ommoord when the weather's good enough. On better days, I channel my frustration into learning new skate tricks. On less good days, I smoke pot and get into fights with the other guys at the skate park.

On those bad days, I hardly recognize myself. So whatever happened to *steezy* (stylin' and easy) living? The more tension in my life, the more competitive I get and the less joy there is in my skating.

Board (snow, surf, or skate) riding is just *not* about winning. But on the bad days I start to take my skill and stick it to people rather than simply enjoying it. I want to be the best at something my dad despises. Rather than sharing waves here at *La Graviere,* I get all aggro and drop in on people—because I can.

I'm not sure how I arrived at this skill level. My memory is so foggy right now. Did I just spend more time riding boards than everyone else? Or was I born with special balance? The truth is, until I got to *La Graviere,* I've always owned every place I've ever ridden. I just totally show up wherever I am, and that seems to be the secret to everything. I don't live in the past—my heart never goes there. Dropping in on a wave here on a big day, you have to have laser-like focus on the present split-second if you want to survive. You can't afford to evaluate or wonder what people will think.

When I was a kid, I was seen as a prodigy. Now that I'm older, I'm seen as a threat, especially by peers. My vibe has gotten twisted. My biggest task in life is figuring out what to do about that. Do I tone it down to become more popular, or go for it with my skills and make them all hate me?

The better I get, the more people want me to go away. Max, for instance, seems genuinely interested in me as a person, but I can tell my increasing skill level deeply troubles him.

When you start to stick out ahead of people, they try to find ways, together, to pull you back to their level. There are all kinds of rules to follow if you want people to like you, and one of them is avoiding excellence that makes anyone else look bad. The rules seem to be especially complex here in France. Ironically, the better I surf here, the less popular I become. For the first time in life, I feel at risk socially. It's not a good feeling.

Oma Adri has no rules for me, but she also doesn't provide any cash, so I have to think twice about each euro I spend. I've had to work at the Not-So-Classic Surf Shop, prepping rental boards. Why does everything in Hossegor have an English name? Oma gave me the choice this summer: (1) She'd give me ample spending money (she has plenty of it!), but I'd have to follow her rules, or (2) She and I would treat each other as adults, but I'd have to come up with my own money. I took door number two, obviously.

I greet a large group of people my age on my way toward the water at sunrise; they are preparing for an all-day party around one of the beach fire pits. I know most of the people. They don't return my greeting with much warmth.

As I wade into the surf at the beach, I can see there are already quite a few surfers in the lineup. You can surf going left or going right on most peaky beachbreak waves, and I almost always go left, since I am left-handed and have a goofy-foot stance. This gives me more wave opportunities, since I can face the wave going left. You don't want to turn your back (i.e., going backside) on the wave face at *La Graviere*. She can hurt you.

But today, I may try to cheat her. True malice wells up inside me—for perhaps the first time in my life. Not just bad judgment but literally the will to hurt someone. I have to do some damage, and Max will do as a target. Nailing a stranger wouldn't do the job. I'm out for blood.

After a tough paddle out (I had to duck dive with my board under the waves seven times to get out to the lineup), I'm sitting on my board and realize that because the wave is so heavy today, I didn't even see the additional half dozen guys out here. There he is. Max is one of them. I always post up to the left of him, because he likes to go right, and crossing paths could be deadly out here.

We nod at each other but say nothing. The less you say in the lineup, the cooler you are.

Oma has known Max and his family for many years. In fact, they have a special relationship that, at times, makes me jealous. Her French is better than mine, so she gets all the humor and irony in Max's stories. I feel foolish when they are laughing together about something I'm clueless about. I party with Max and his gang, and go to church and read books with Oma. I'd like to keep those worlds separate, but Max and Oma keep forcing them together. Both of them have a hard edge, and they have been known to turn it on me. Yet, even with these two huge personalities knee-deep in my soul, I'm starting to feel lonely here at Hossegor.

This past weekend the three of us had dinner at our home, and they were trading mocking impersonations of me fumbling through French pick-up lines. I started getting hot behind my eyes and began plotting revenge. I can get along with either one of them individually, but when they are together, I feel like a foreigner to the only two people in Hossegor who supposedly care about me.

Today I am going to stick him. Slowly, but deliberately, I make a decision. I cross an invisible line that no one else can see me cross. My body starts to tingle with anticipation.

The waves are so loud that we can't hear each other, even in shouting. Max points to the outside. My knees go weak. It's the universal sign for "a big one coming outside." We paddle like crazy for the horizon. If we don't make it up the face of the oncoming wave before it breaks, it will simply break us.

As usual, Max and I, always totally aware of each other's position, pivot precisely to face the beach at the critical second and are set to go right and left off the peak of the wave. We call it "splitting the peak" and have done it countless times. The drop will be down the face of the wave, almost two stories high. Everyone else paddles over the crest in deference to us—the silent pecking order at heavy surf breaks. Exactly at the tipping moment, Max paddles into the wave, going right, as always. It's so heavy, he's barely going to make the drop. He expects me to go left, but I decide to betray him.

I brought my gun, a big-wave board that paddles faster than his shortboard. I pivot not left, but right, and out-paddle him, just behind and downhill from him, where he can't see me, and then slingshot myself past him on my right rail, crouched and grabbing my left rail with my hand to hold my line on the steep face of the wave.

I commit the unthinkable mortal surfing sin. I cut him off on a double-overhead wave. Nietzsche's phrase "will to power" shoots through my mind, and my heart goes a deep black. I hear Max scream behind me as he pitches off his board and into the wave headfirst. I shoot forward, racing backside on the thundering wave face.

No one else on the coast of France today could pull off what I just did, turning my back on *La Graviere* and living to tell about it. And I did it with authority. I feel a rush of mixed emotions. Elation for catching the wave and flying backside to the right. A visceral pushback against my father. Anger at Max for mocking me with Oma Adri. Horror and guilt at what I have just done. Anger at God for setting up a no-win game in life. Fear at what awaits me from Max's friends on the beach. Deep regret, knowing that Max may be in serious trouble.

Max will be stuck underwater for at least two waves, trapped in the turbulence and unable to breathe. If his leash breaks, he might drown. I can't paddle back to the lineup with his friends there. And he has even more friends, people with whom he grew up, on the beach, sitting around a fire, preparing for the vacation parties of the day. I never exactly thought through what I would do in this situation if I succeeded.

As I reach the sand and bend over to undo the ankle Velcro from my leash, the friends of Max, both in the water and on the beach, split into two groups. One searches for him in the turbulence and then helps him and his broken board out of the water, and one group comes after me, cursing me in French.

There is nowhere to run. I don't even try. Locals around here have been waiting to explode on this outsider for quite some time.

I take my deserved beating. Just like at the African church, I black out and hit the ground. But this time, it isn't prayer that does it to me. It's pure physical violence I've brought upon myself. For an instant, I have the obviously false impression that I'm tied helplessly to an iron gate as I take hit after hit. I go fetal, hoping to live through it.

In the end, it is Max—still shaking from the fear of a near drowning and gasping for air, running toward us out of the water—who stops them from going too far.

~ Behind the Story ~
Angelo

5 May 1945
Liberation Day
Hillegersberg, Holland

It's a year after Ruud and Nellie's town hall wedding. The flowers in the gardens everywhere are glorious. No one does flowers like the Dutch.

There is euphoria in the air. The Germans have just quit all claim to Holland. Who would have believed it? But there is also an uneasiness floating around. The multitudes of Dutch citizens who supported the Germans, at whatever level, are all holding their breath and keeping a low profile. Most are wisely staying home.

Nellie is not so wise. She comes around the corner pushing a pram. I want to look inside and see the baby, of course, but now is not the time.

A crowd approaches from the other direction.

Nellie stops a few feet away, absolutely frozen. The blood drains from her face as she sees the angry mob approaching from a block away.

I break all the rules and pull myself into her world. Sometimes it just has to be done.

I jump up to the pram. "I'll take little Adri for you. You can trust me. I'm a friend," I say to Nellie.

Briefly shaking off the fear, Nellie kisses the baby girl on the forehead and asks, "How did you know her name?" Then she hands her to me and screams, "Run! Run! RUN!"

I run with the baby. Like the wind. I can't see the mob anymore as I race away with little Adri, searching for safety.

But I have my sources, and I'll tell you what happened. What follows is intense.

The crowd is not interested in the baby. They want Nellie.

And at the front and center of the approaching crowd is… her mother.

1945

Hillegersberg, Holland

PEK EN VEREN (tar and feathers).

The crowd carries the terrified and struggling Nellie through the graveyard and up toward the Hillegonda church. The gag is so tight on her mouth that she can hardly breathe.

No. Not there. Not where I met Walter. O God, no, she thinks and prays. The forces of evil always seem to do their ugliest work in the holiest places.

Another group is waiting for them at the iron gate by the door next to the blackberry bush.

At the top of the gate is a hand-painted sign: VERRADER (traitor).

The thick stench of boiling tar fills her nostrils as they slam Nellie's writhing body onto the iron of the gate, opening a big wound on the back of her head. She almost blacks out from the concussion.

The blood flows freely down her back as they rope her arms to the bars.

No, that can't be a barber's shaving razor! she thinks groggily. *No...oh no...O God, no.*

Two men, with great force, hold her head still as the blade scrapes across her scalp. She stops struggling so the blade will cut into her skin less. Since she is gagged, she can only scream silently with all her might. Thick piles of shiny hair fall in clumps all around her, with some skin attached here and there.

Paintbrushes full of hot tar scald her skin as someone rips her shirt off, and the black, steaming, roofing pitch is lapped onto her. Someone smears a cooler, clumpy handful of it right on her face, grinding it into her perfect features.

Nellie is shaking with fear. *If I can keep one of my nostrils clear, I can survive*, she thinks. *Just keep breathing, Nellie girl. Just keep breathing. Do it for baby Adri. She needs you.*

The big razor is then used to cut open three pillows, and the feathers are dumped on her.

A huge cheer of jubilation goes up. People are laughing. *Laughing!* The mob starts ridiculing her with shouts of "Sieg Heil!" and Hitler salutes.

She closes her eyes so she won't have to see the mocking, taunting faces of her neighbors... many of whom she has grown up with. It's too ugly to watch.

A woman's small hand grabs her jaw, and Nellie is able to open only one eye. The other has tarred itself shut.

Her mother's face is inches from hers. "Don't ever come home again!" she screams and spits in Nellie's face.

That's the last thing Nellie sees before she passes out to jeering chants of *"MOF-FEN-MEID! MOF-FEN-MEID!"*

...Kraut Girl...

*

2008

Melrose District

Los Angeles, California

Kati

ONCE AGAIN I'M AVOIDING GOING HOME. I'm standing up, straddling my beach cruiser, browsing the magazines at the outdoor newsstand right here in the middle of the Melrose District.

Later, I can swing around to the street behind mine and hang out with Zara's family this evening. Mutti would never dream of showing up there, and she simply can't make me come home tonight if I don't want to.

I'm a legal adult now and make plenty of money working for Zara's uncle in his chain of convenience stores. This gives me some independence.

I've dodged Mutti's attempts to get me to cut my hair for five years now, and she's horrified at how it looks. I won't even trim the ends. I like it wild and bushy and almost down to my waist—it makes me look bigger than my skinny self. Sometimes I braid it so it won't get caught in things. But most of the time, I keep it under control and out of my face with a whole line of different-colored men's fedoras that I pick up at swap meets. I still have all the big sunglasses. I look like a tall, skinny Karen O.

The chain of events leading from my DUI down to today has left me without access to a car, but who really needs that here in the district? It's only three in the afternoon, and I've been thinking about drinking several times already today. When you're as lean as I am, it doesn't take much alcohol to push you all the way over the edge.

I'm still waiting for the first young man to pay any attention to me in "that way." There are more of us than you think.

For prom night a few months ago, a bunch of us "left behinds" went shopping for retro formal gowns at a thrift store, did wild makeup, and had a slumber party at one of the girls' homes, drinking way too much and dancing our brains out. Her parents seemed sad somehow about hosting the event but worked with us to help make it happen.

I'm convinced by now that many parents carry a chronic deep disappointment in their kids around with them for decades. You can see it in their eyes. I can see it in Mutti. With her, there is a flash of anger mixed in with the disappointment about me. I think she was mad at me before I was born. She's angry at me because no one asked me to prom. Angry at *me*.

I woke up in the middle of the night at the prom party and stepped over bodies in sleeping bags to get to the bathroom. I turned the water and the fan on, sat on the toilet lid with my head in my hands, my wild, loose hair covering most of me like a big thicket, and sobbed so hard it was difficult to stop. Then I washed off my ruined makeup and went back to my sleeping bag....

I awaken from my not-so-pleasant memories when I drop the magazine I'm browsing through at the newsstand.

How can the whole zero-male-attention thing throw my self-esteem into a sticky, urban trash can? I try to ease up on myself, but underneath I wonder, *Am I really that ugly?*

Opa's been gone for a couple of years now, and for the longest time before his passing, he wasn't able to interact much. It's like he died a little bit at a time. I check my watch now, which makes me think of him. Tonight I'm going to do something that will push Mutti across the line, but I want to do it to remember Opa.

I look at my tattoo-free right wrist for one of the last times ever. I purposely am going to get ink that goes up high on the back of my hand, almost to my knuckles, so it will be hard to cover with a sleeve. It's edgy and will go well with my untrimmed hair.

Seems like everything I do has mixed motives. Truth is, I'm doing this to spite Mutti *and* to remember a dear grandfather. Are there any motives in life that aren't mixed? I doubt it. The more pressure I feel from the outside, the more broken my motives are. The demands of life are simply impossible…and I'm living proof.

I've been doodling versions of our Dornbusch family coat of arms for much of my life: the heart with the crown of thorns around it. I brought my best sketches to Mama Mahala at Kupina Tattoo on Melrose, and she re-did three options for me. Yesterday we agreed on one. Black thorns, letters, and a red heart. I'm putting the German Gothic letters *HWD* in the center heart for Opa's full name: Harald Walter Dornbusch.

I've also decided I'm not going to USC this fall.

Like someone like me wants to go to a private school like USC anyway with perfect young people from prosperous families. It would be a dream come true for Mutti, of course. But organized education has never worked for me—at least socially. Except for meeting Zara at school, most of my friends grew up with me at church.

Hope Lutheran Church on Melrose is one of the few places I feel totally at home, even without Opa. We had a long talk the first time he wasn't physically able to go with me on a Sunday morning. When I offered to stay home with him, he pulled me down to his chair. I remembered sadly when he was always able to stand out of respect for me. Not anymore. Placing his old but aristocratic hands on both sides of my head, Opa kissed me on the forehead and made me promise I'd take my grandkids to church someday.

"If you go every Sunday after I'm gone," Opa said, "it's a way for us to spend time together. Someday you'll understand. But for now, you have the special-needs kids who are counting on you this morning. Bless you, darling princess." He kissed my forehead for a second time, and off I went on my bike.

His last gift to me was a large Asian teakwood winder case with padded wrists inside that silently rotate with electric engines and thereby wind all of the automatic mechanical watches from the sea chest, which keeps them in better condition. They are worth a fortune to collectors. But they are worth much more than that to me. Mutti hates it when I wear them, and I always suspect she is going to try to hide them from me—or worse. The Ziffer alone is worth almost a million dollars to collectors.

I miss Opa's constant encouragement. He would have been proud, seeing me the day I graduated from high school. I was just glad to be done and out of there. The only reason I go back to Fairfax High School now is for the Melrose Trading Post held there every Sunday afternoon. Hippest swap meet in the universe. I swing by on my bike every week on the way home from church.

It's the best afternoon of my week. My heart usually sings all the way to the Trading Post because of the magic that happens in my class at church on Sunday mornings. I've been working with three of the four children in my special-needs Sunday school class for several years now. The fourth one is new to the group. Their families come to the church because of my work there. They often invite me to their homes for birthdays and holidays. We are starting to work out plans for my permanent work with the kids, and I'm *really* excited about it. I can't think of a job I'd ever love more.

My four students never expect anything from me. They take me just the way I am. With Opa passing slowly, the hopeless situation with Mutti, and tensions with Zara building over our diverging lives, I've been taking every opportunity to work with my kids and their families.

I find myself, for the first time today, here at the newsstand, avoiding going to Zara's house.

Why am I hesitating?

It all started at Yosemite National Park a few weeks ago at the beginning of summer after our graduation from Fairfax High School. Zara's parents invited me to go with them. They had reservations in the Ahwahnhee Hotel.

They have "made it" in America and are starting to enjoy showing it. Nice cars. Always a little overdressed. Her dad wears shirts that are a bit too tight, an Asian way of showing you have plenty to eat. At Yosemite, her mother wore traditional Pakistani clothing with American designer shoes. It's hard to figure out exactly what the rules are for Zara's clothing, especially since she started to blossom as a young woman. It seems like they are so proud of her looking and dressing American but have her go traditional at family events at home.

In any case, Zara looked stunning that day in Yosemite. It was probably the most beautiful day of her life. We all have one of those. God forbid mine has already passed. She wore shorts, flip-flops, and a bright orange top. Her skin was perfect. Her almost-black hair, unlike my massive frizz, was shiny and lying perfectly.

But it was her eyes and teeth that shone out from her royally shaped face with dark skin that made her nearly too beautiful to look at. Her luminous, big brown eyes were outlined with heavily emphasized eyeliner. My smile is good, but nothing like Zara's was on that day. It would be impossible for any man to walk past her without sneaking a look. Just strolling along in the pine-scented sunshine with her promenading family, she was like a weightless dancer in perfect balance.

We all (Zara's uncle had brought his family too) walked up the paved path to Yosemite Falls. We were quite a sight with a dozen people, including me. Suddenly having trouble breathing because of all the compound jealousy and anxiety, I figured that if I could get out ahead of them, I wouldn't have to look at Zara. I was feeling choked up in the throat as I walked forward, looking down, even though the Yosemite Falls—one of the most spectacular sights in all of nature—was right ahead of me and up high. Even more, it's hard to walk with my head down, because my big mop of hair falls forward and I can't see much, even with my fedora. So I tossed my head back and kept walking, looking up at the falls.

Putting space between myself and the group, I turned and glanced back at them. A very average family with a physically stunning daughter in the very peak hour of her life.

Turning back to face front, I stumbled through a group of about six boys my age, tanned and muscular, walking the opposite way. Two of them were carrying skateboards. Frat types. Confident. Wealthy.

I'll never forget the words of the obvious team captain as he stopped right next to me, as if I didn't exist, and stared at Zara: "Guys! Look…at…her."

I started to run. Faster and faster.

Turning right at the base of the lower falls, the trail goes over a stone bridge. I climbed over the stone rail and clambered down onto the boulders that led to the base of the falls and started working toward the spray.

No one is ever going to notice me. The thought hit hard. Panic, frustration, and anger spurred me on. One boulder at a time, I kept climbing. At last I had to stop. I was out of breath.

Suddenly, there was a hand on my left shoulder.

Saahir. The son of Zara's uncle. We'd worked a few shifts together in the chain of convenience stores. He looks like a chubby forty-five-year-old, even though he's my age. He always dresses too old. But he's steady as the day is long. And bright. And kind.

"I thought I would run on ahead and see the falls with you, Kati," he said quietly that day....

Completing my mental walk down Memory Lane, I realize I'm just stalling. Finally I leave the magazine racks of the convenience store and hop back on my bike to head for Zara's house. Riding up the narrow driveway leading to the garage behind the stucco house, I park my bike, inhale the aroma of curry, and go in through the back door. I've had a key for years but don't need it today. The men are sitting on the back patio.

The older men in the extended family are observant Muslims. No alcohol and no foolishness. Shrewd businessmen, they see the opportunities of buying up gas stations in sketchier neighborhoods where others are reticent to do business, converting them to upgraded convenience stores, and creating cash flow. Something tells me that their projects are going to be a part of my life for a long time.

Zara's aunt—Saahir's mother—and I have developed a special relationship. She's at Zara's house almost every day. She seems to love me almost as much as Opa did. We spend hours together in the kitchen. Her English is atrocious, and she appreciates any help I can give tutoring her. Because I speak several languages, I know how to talk in such a way as to be easily understood.

Strange, but these days I come here more to see her than to be with Zara.

Zara will be off to school at Cal Poly San Luis Obispo in the fall. I'll have to go see her on the train if I can't get my driver's license back.

I stop daydreaming and find myself in the kitchen, preparing dinner with my "aunt," looking out the window onto the narrow residential street while chopping food. Zara drives up in a convertible with two guys, all of them laughing a little too loud. Unlike me, most Anglos are a little nervous about coming into a Pakistani house, so Zara comes in alone.

Just realized that I haven't told Mutti where I am. I start to smile because I know that will bother her. When was the last time I thought of my father? He takes up almost no space in my head, even though he lives in the house with us.

Saahir is out on the back porch with the men, explaining how the new accounting software works. They have started to depend on his judgment. He's a funny little man, and I think he arranges his days so he can see more of me....

After dinner, Zara and I glance at each other, smile, and realize it's time. We do the ritual good-bye greetings with the whole houseful, put on our hoodie sweatshirts, and head out for Kupina Tattoo, a few blocks away.

I am so excited; there are huge butterflies in my stomach.

On the way we chat, and I forgive her in my heart for the Yosemite incident, even though she has no idea it even happened or how it devastated me. Zara is a nondisposable friend. A sister. And you can't divorce a sister.

We were junior high friends who liked art. She blossomed and I didn't. Will I ever? Would we still have become friends if we met now? We started at the same starting line, but she is now lapping me—over and over. Who knows?

Soon we're standing in front of Mama Mahala at Kupina Tattoo. Mama looks me straight in the eyes and asks, pointing down at the final design on paper, "Are you sure, young lady? How about farther up the arm so a long sleeve will cover it for formal occasions?"

I pull out Opa's Pelikan fountain pen and sign the release. I slap a pile of cash down on the counter with authority.

"No," I say. "All the way up to the base of my knuckles. It's my money. It's my right hand. It was my grandfather. Do it. Now."

It's hideous. And beautiful. Just as I had hoped.

It's so sore. So very sore.

I miss you, Opa.

~ BEHIND THE STORY ~
Angelo

Ever notice that with a dream or a daydream, you can be gone for hours, and only miss a few minutes?

The last we heard, Nellie was being tarred and feathered. But there's so much more of the story....

Back to 1982
Bijenkorf Department Store
Rotterdam, Holland

Nellie and Janine

NELLIE PULLS OUT A TINY BOX. Janine opens it and retrieves an exotic gold ring with multiple rubies in it. The rubies form a crown.

"I got this from Ruud when we were living in Asia," Oma Nellie says. "Ruud is pure faithfulness. The best man I ever knew. A man of family wealth and reputation who made a second fortune on his own in Asia with me. We were a formidable couple. When we were together, I would feel power all around us.

"Here, Janine, I want you to have it. Wear it and let it remind you of the secret I'm about to share with you. A secret Ruud wanted you to know about, but I wanted to wait until you were a young woman."

Nellie takes a breath, suddenly nervous. "Ruud is not your physical grandfather. Let me tell you about a man named Walter. He was the love of my life. Your face, Janine, *Je lijkt sprekend op hem* (you look just like him). You remind me of him every day.

"My love for you, my dear grandchild, is, in a manner of speaking, the only way I can live out my love for him without hurting others. Walter passed away a few years ago, but he always asked about you. I sent him many pictures of you, which he had to keep hidden. Ruud knew about Walter, but Walter's wife…well, she was never told."

Nellie pulls out a familiar winter picture of a younger Janine eating (fried potato cakes with applesauce—what the locals call *Reibekuchen*) outside the Cologne Cathedral.

"Do you remember, a few years ago, when I took this picture of you and that nice man we met outside the Cologne train station? He posed for a picture with you. I could barely hold the camera; my hands were shaking so badly. Do you see the resemblance in your faces? This is the only picture of you together with your grandfather Walter. You had no idea who he really was. You asked me why I handed the man an old wristwatch; I made up some excuse to satisfy your curiosity.

"Ever since his return from Russia, we had met secretly a few times. The day you were with me was one of those precious times. It was also the day I gave his treasured Ziffer à Grand Complication 1924 watch back to him—the one he'd given me for safekeeping while he was away in Russia. I knew, somehow, that he should have it back."

A single tear gathers on the rim of Nellie's eyelashes. "I sent him the picture of the two of you, and he wrote later to say he would someday arrange to have a copy of the picture secretly tucked inside his German officer's uniform jacket when he was buried. He always wanted this picture next to his heart."

Nellie struggles with her next words. Her voice moves to a whisper. "That day with you in Cologne was the last time I ever saw him in person. Janine, even though I was totally faithful to dear Ruud since we married, for me, Walter was the one. Our letters helped us work through all we had been through during that hellacious time of war and rebuilding…."

Nellie seems lost in memory for a moment before she continues.

"A mysterious person delivered your mother, baby Adri, to Ruud's mother, Tante Riek, at their Hillegersberg home on the darkest day of my life," Oma Nellie explains to Janine. "Riek said that, after handing Adri over, the messenger vanished into thin air. Literally. Not running or walking away...simply vanishing.

"Your Opa Ruud found me, his young wife, half-unconscious and tied to the black-iron church gate. He had promised to protect me, but he came too late. He carried me home."

As Janine's jaw drops in shock, Nellie goes back over the details of the *pek en veeren* incident and then continues.

"No hospital would take me in, given the political climate at the close of the War, so my family secured the services of a doctor brave enough, despite social pressure, to care for me at my in-laws' home.

"The first night was touch and go. The necessary scraping of the tar from my skin added to the trauma, and I drifted in and out of shock. The back of my head needed stitches, and I had numerous burns on my body."

Taking Janine's perfect young hands in hers over the restaurant table, Nellie sighs. "What a relief it was to wake up the next morning and realize I was fully able to breathe. And to see Ruud's faithful eyes! How troubled they were, how pained...and, yes, how angry as well. But his touch on my brow was infinitely loving."

Nellie swallows hard. "I had no idea, until much later, how intensely he suffered with me during that time, or how, for years, he would wrestle with the injustice of what happened...dear Ruud. So kind always." Her voice and hands tremble.

"In my very first words that morning, my maternal instincts deep within commanded me to ask, '*Waar is Adri?* (Where is Adri?)' Then Ruud's mother told me the whole story about the disappearing messenger while she brought in baby Adri for me to cuddle."

~ BEHIND THE STORY ~
Angelo

Eventually, Nellie and Ruud would share a huge apartment in Ommoord, Holland, where they raised Adri as a teen. It was at the top of a postwar apartment building and took up the whole floor. The 360-degree view was magnificent. The elevator opened directly into their living room—you needed a key to get to that floor.

To the north and west, you could see across the Rotte River to Hillegersberg. On a clear day, the IJssel and Maas rivers were visible. To the north were soggy, deep green pastures with black and white cows hemmed in by countless canals. You could almost feel the industrial hum from the bustling port of Rotterdam, only a bike ride away. Around them, high-rise apartments were under construction for decades.

Ruud and Nellie had spent the first ten years after the War abroad in Asia, and when they returned, they chose this new town of Ommoord, arising out of farmland on the outskirts of Rotterdam.

They couldn't go back to live in Hillegersberg, because Nellie had, along with a plethora of folks, been *fout in de oorlog* ("mistaken" in the War—collaborating or fraternizing with the enemy), and it was too hard for her to see any of the town or its people ever again.

When an enemy army occupies your nation and you cooperate with them at any level, you roll the dice. If they stay, you win. If they are expelled, you lose big.

Nellie played the grand piano in that penthouse apartment every single day. She knew Chopin's preludes by heart. Janine could still play "Für Elise" on the piano at the Methodist church in Zarzamora, since Nellie had taught it to her back in Ommoord.

Nellie would often sing when she played the piano. Her voice was deep, resonant, and haunting. It sent out a kind of authority.

And she would sing psalms *a cappella* in the morning while making coffee. She would sign her birthday cards to her grand-daughter, Janine, with psalm references.

The three of them, Nellie, Ruud, and Adri, would go to church together in a smallish warehouse in the middle of Ommoord. The little flock was Pentecostal and independent, not like the established Reformed church in Hillegersberg. It was a safe church for social outsiders. Immigrants. Those who had been *fout* in the War and all kinds of uninhibited spirits in this most buttoned-down of societies: Anyone wired a little differently. A simple big sign was painted on the side of the warehouse: KOM EN ZIE (Come and see). They would sometimes break into dance and spontaneous singing during worship.

Adri was less exuberant. She would often sit quietly during these explosions of expression. But very early on in her teens, the congregation recognized that Adri had a special gift.

She could speak for God.

This was a congregation that embraced Adri's gift of the prophetic. The prophet Joel had written, long before Christ, that "your sons and your daughters shall prophesy" (2:28).

Adri had one mood and one only: focused and present. And only one expression on her face: attention. She was always, even as an adult, tiny as a bird; perhaps because of prenatal and early childhood wartime malnourishment. Never would she break eye contact with anyone first. After a while, during a conversation with her, people had to look away, just for a respite from the intensity of looking at her flaming eyes.

The penthouse apartment was home to the multi-generational family that raised Janine and was in a constant flurry of activity. Piano. Bicycling every day. Cocktail parties for dignitaries who came—partly just to be seen with Ruud, partly to enjoy the spectacular view. Churchgoing. And, for Janine, school.

Ruud would take the train to work in The Hague. He would manage the old money from the family and the new money he had made in Asia.

Nellie was very entrenched in her new life, but she could never forget the German officer whom she had loved...the father of her baby....

1979
Oberwinter am Rhein, Germany
Just south of Bonn

Walter

WALTER IS READY TO DIE, and he knows the time is short. He has put on his military uniform from decades ago. Still has perfect posture and great dignity. He is standing in front of an open sea chest.

Just this morning and just in time, he received the registered package from Nellie of all the letters he has ever written her, knowing it is time to lock the entire story away for another generation, in due time, to discover and learn. Didn't the prophet Daniel do something similar?

He and Nellie have both decided that Harald will be the one best suited to handle the contents of the sea chest. Adri is too unpredictable.

Neatly arranging the contents of the chest, Walter takes his favorite picture of all—the one of his granddaughter, Janine, in Cologne—and places it inside his vest pocket. He knows his eyes will close for the last time before seeing it again. But he is ready.

One last task before closing and locking the chest. Walter removes the Ziffer watch from his wrist, places it in the special Asian-wood watch cabinet with the others; then he seals it. It's doubtful anyone else in the family will appreciate elite watches as he does, Walter thinks.

Twenty-four hours from now, he guesses, the last of the watches will run out of spring tension and stop ticking. He doubts his heart will still be pumping by then. The doctors are amazed he is still alive. His lungs never recovered from Russia.

He signs one final note to his son, Walter, with a quote from Bertold Brecht: *Denk an uns mit Nachsicht.*

He closes the chest for the last time and kneels beside it. He mouths the simple prayer of Luke 23:42 out loud:

> *Jesu, HERR, gedenke an mich, wenn du in dein Reich kommst* (Jesus, Lord, remember me when thou comest into thy kingdom)!

He stands and puts a huge padlock on the sea chest, locks it, and puts the key in his coat pocket.

Then he walks downstairs to die in peace.

~ BEHIND THE STORY ~

Angelo

Back to 1982

Bijenkorf Department Store

Rotterdam, Holland

Nellie still is remarkably beautiful. She's also very active, riding her bike to all of her errands daily. She's never learned to drive. Even as an older grandmother, she draws the attention of everyone in the room. The notch in her eyebrow and the scar along her jaw from her tar-and-feathers experience haven't put a dent in her elegance. She is regal.

Her thick hair has grown back in nicely and covers most of the razor scars; she wears it in a swooping, elegant updo to mask the small, bare patches. Janine is one of the only people who ever saw her grandmother's hair down—and her scars and bare spots. Nellie lets her brush it out and put it back up.

Nellie's eyes now shimmer with tears. "That I can sit across from such a wonderful young woman as you, today, who reminds me so much of Walter, is proof that God has forgiven me."

Janine holds the ring with the tips of fingers from both hands, then slips it onto her right ring finger. A perfect fit. Her eyes well up. The gold and rubies start to blur. Her thoughts likewise blur. Pain, atrocity, cruelty, *fout in de oorlog*, shame, faithfulness, secrets, the "one." It's a lot for a sixteen-year-old to handle.

Janine glances once again at the ring box and the birthday card resting on top.

"Just a minute," Oma Nellie says and pulls out her Mont Blanc fountain pen from her purse. Taking the card, she writes in elegant script, *Psalm 51.*

September 11, 2001
Zarzamora, California

Janine

JANINE SHUDDERS BACK INTO REALITY at the Zarzamora Winery.
No one is there.
She looks down at her right hand, laid out flat on the bar.
And sees the rubies set in gold.
Deep calleth out to deep....

PART THREE

2011

Huntington Beach, California

Josh

THE U.S. OPEN OF SURFING IS FINALLY HERE, and up until this morning, I was in the running for the trophy.

Not that I had much of a shot at the $100,000 first-place prize, but this thing is called "Open" because it's...well...open. Days and days of qualifying and heats. Intense boredom punctuated by moments of great intensity. On any given day, the right wave could come along, and...you just never know. Local boy Brett Simpson knocked out world champion Mick Fanning back in '09, and Jordy Smith in '10.

This place is an anthill. Three hundred thousand people are all over downtown Huntington Beach. Airplanes pull huge beer-ad trailers back and forth across the cloudless blue sky. The festival at the beach is free. Bands. Booths. Motorcycles doing flips in midair. The ubiquitous smell of coconut-scented sunscreen. Skateboard competitions. Beach volleyball nets in neat rows as far as the eye can see. Flat, tanned stomachs everywhere you look. Packs of young women glowing in the sunshine; packs of young men on the hunt.

I come out of the water with my Quiet Flite shortboard (how

I ended up on a board from Florida is another story—but it's a sweet ride) and look up at the stands, set up like a NASCAR race, and pull my neon-colored competition vest off. South African prodigy Jordy Smith comes over and fist-bumps me, and the crowd stands and cheers as he holds his board over his head after a hard-fought victory. Autograph seekers mob him at the waterline. There may be a couple of days of tough competition ahead of him if he wants to win this thing.

There is a high wave advisory out today; they needed jet skis to get us out to the lineup. The biggest waves are almost lapping the deck of the pier and occasionally spraying the crowd watching from the guardrail. The big waves were to my advantage, since my home break in France is the legendary *La Graviere*. I hope all the tourists stay out of the water. It's deadly dangerous.

The judges have punched in their numbers, and my name is at the bottom on the JumboTron. That shouldn't bother me, but it does. My dad was obsessed with scores. Most adults carry around numbers their whole lives. Social Security numbers. Credit ratings. Passwords. Net worth. You name it. And when this stuff gets stolen, they call it "identity theft." Like someone can steal your identity.

They list me as *FRA* (French) up on the big scoreboard, even though I'm an American citizen. I came up through the ranks at Hossegor, and they want to make this thing look like some global World Cup or something.

My bros are gathered at the waterline. What a crew: Max. Sam. The rest. Max greets me with a French obscenity—his usual. Sam yells out "J-Bro!" Oma Adri is with them. She kisses me on both cheeks and insists on about ten pictures of all of us—even making me put my neon-colored competition vest back on. When Adri commands, everyone obeys. Max, coming from a wealthy family, can travel without worrying about it—he never thought twice about flying all the way from France to watch me.

Oma's three times older than anyone else in the whole U.S. Open crowd but somehow fits in, wearing cooler sunglasses than anyone else. Oma Adri, in a trait she got from her mother, Nellie, owns any group she's in or any room she enters. She insists on treating us all to lunch across the Pacific Coast Highway at TK Burger, but we have to swim upstream through the massive festival crowd on the beach to get there.

The sand is biting hot on our feet, and bikini-clad promo girls hand everyone huge, shiny-canned, free-sample energy drinks out of ice-filled barrels.

A typical blond California girl about my age I've never, ever seen before bolts in from my left, apparently seeing my competition vest and board, and plants a huge wet kiss on my lips; she tastes and smells heavily of beer, even before lunch. She messes up my hair and runs off to her friends. I don't even have time to react. Oma teases me by messing up my hair again and making fun of the girl's running gait. This gets a huge laugh from my friends, of course.

We work our way through the dozens of promo booths—it's kind of like a state fair on steroids. We have to move out of the way for a pack of young women heading for the water. The exotic dark-skinned one in the front is simply breathtakingly magnetic and flashes a perfect smile at us. She turns and says something to a vaguely familiar skinny friend with a big nose behind her, who laughs in response.

I brush shoulders with the skinny one in the crush of the crowd, and something tingles in the pit of my stomach. Is she really wearing a fedora hat and a large men's watch? Odd. The pack squeezes past us, and I strain to get another look at the attractive one, who looks like she's from India or something.

Too late.

Oma looks troubled.

"The crowds bothering you?" I ask her in Dutch, so as not to embarrass her.

"No," she says, "there's just something...something... I don't know what it is."

I put my arm around her, and we continue making our way to lunch.

*

2011
The Cliffs
Huntington Beach, California

Kati

WELL, I'VE WALKED FAR ENOUGH, and my eyes are still stinging. My throat is burning with anger, disappointment, grief, jealousy, and a healthy dose of depression. It's so hard to keep from looking like a fool with beet-red eyes when you're walking north along the beach where so many people can see you. Most of the time, no one is looking at you, but a day like today is *all about* looking.

I've never figured out how to have a non-awkward walk, and the more I think about it, the more awkward my gait becomes. When Zara walks, boys just start following. She just sort of swings and smiles as she goes.

I give up.

Not only can't I compete, I can't even suit up for the game. My head is hot. I remove my fedora and toss it to a teenage boy walking the opposite direction, smiling tentatively at him.

He catches it and looks puzzled. "Whatever, lady," he snarls at me.

Great. He discards it on the ground next to him and moves on.

I just want to do something meaningful in life and have a better family than the one in which I grew up. Is that too much to ask?

Zara has no idea where I am. She was having so much fun basking in all the attention that she didn't even notice my leaving. An hour from now, she'll think, *Where's Kati?*

Put a fork in me—I'm done.

It's just one too many times to have to endure the same thing. Guys congregate around Zara and I disappear. Replayed a bazillion times. What a stupid idea to go with her to the U.S. Open. Thousands of girls our age in swimsuits, and she's at the top of the hot list. Me? I'm in negative numbers. I had to go for a walk to clear my head, but it feels like the emotional clouds are gathering. And I can't do anything to stop them.

I've been drinking so much this week; at this rate, I'll never get my driver's license back. The buzz is keeping me from thinking through what I'm doing right now. It feels unreal somehow. I keep checking my Ziffer watch as evening approaches to keep myself grounded in reality.

Evening is on the way. What if morning never comes?

Now there's a thought. *Get a grip on yourself, girl,* I tell myself. But I know I'm losing my grip.

The beach is narrowing the farther north I go. The Huntington Beach Cliffs are rising on my right.

*

Simultaneously
Bolsa Chica Beach
Huntington Beach, California

Josh

It's been a cruisy afternoon and evening, and the sun is about to set. My surf sponsor, Quiet Flite, arranged a spot up here a few miles north of the competition for some R and R. They have a big advertising-wrapped RV in the parking lot stocked with all kinds of goodies. Oma left a couple of hours ago, and the mood at our celebration is now starting to take off. The party is focusing around a concrete fire pit.

But me? Well, I'm walking south on the beach, alone, along the waterline toward the Cliffs. The setting sun has lit up the rocks with reds and oranges, and the tide is coming in. I have a touch of sunburn sting, but the wind is picking up and cooling things off nicely. No one is in the water; the surf is too heavy. It's so loud I can barely hear myself think.

And maybe that isn't such a bad thing. Ever since I betrayed Max, back at Hossegor, my life has felt drained dry, as if that event started a soul bleeding that hasn't really stopped. I still can't fathom how—or why—Max stood by me, even after I'd done the unthinkable to him. And he was my *friend.* What if Max had died? What I did was the emotional equivalent of premeditated murder. Max refuses to talk about it...and that makes it even harder for me. His noble reaction is such a contrast to my dark action that I can barely look him in the eyes these days.

The dreams I was having before I betrayed Max have virtually stopped, just when I was so close to mastering them. Now I awaken in the mornings with a blank screen and no dream memories. And a vague sense of being in debt, spiritually and emotionally.

The truth is, I'm taking what God wired into me—special gifts for discerning the present and an almost supernatural sense of balance and focus—and I'm using them to win surf contests. How tacky. It seems like every year, I get more and more entangled in broken responses to impossible demands.

I keep looking at the horizon—can't keep my eyes off of it. Something is wrong; I can feel it. The rest of the world vanishes as I scan the rough waves with eyes trained for years to spot every tiny fluctuation in the water.

But there's no one out there.

Since the day I cut Max off, I've felt like damaged goods. I'm lost around my father. Clueless around my mother—I don't seem to be able to access any of her goodness. I don't have a girlfriend.

Only Adri and Max hang in there with me, willing to go the distance.

*

Kati

THE TIDE IS HIGH, and it's blocked my path forward. No more sand beach. Just crashing waves on the left and rocks on the right. It's getting darker. I should probably climb through the clefts of the moonlit rock on the right to the main path along the Pacific Coast Highway.

Whoa. That wave just rolled past me, and the little remaining sand is crumbling beneath my feet as it washes back. It's like the water lapping around my legs wants to suck me right out into the dark ocean. Is it only me, or is the wind really whipping up too? There are whitecaps on the huge waves out there.

I'm starting to get cold. After all these years, I still have zero body mass; I can never keep warm. If it wasn't for the flowered wrap dress I'm wearing, it would still be hard for people to tell my gender... maybe except for my long braid. My swimsuit top, under the beach wrap, is more or less pointless.

Oh, great. My eyes are starting to burn again because of that now.

Well, I can escape the incoming tide if I climb through the rocks up to the path. In any case, I am NOT going back to the party scene behind me. On the other hand, one way or another I have to try to find Zara, eventually, to get home, since I can't drive. I check my Ziffer 1924 watch; it's almost too dark to read the dials. Zara decided not to bring a phone, because she and all the other perfect girls are wearing virtually nothing and have no pockets, so I can't call her. I may have to call her family. Phone in my wrap dress pocket? Yup.

I certainly don't want to face all of Mutti's questions about how this day has unraveled.

Talk about epic fail.

*

Josh

Is THAT A GIRL trying to climb the Cliffs at high tide? I strain my eyes in the dusky red to see. Probably a girl, because I see a long braid flapping in the wind.

The tide is *so* high. The crashing surf is hammering away and eroding the dirt in the Cliffs.

Everyone, especially my sponsor, is thrilled I got so far in the competition this morning.

But it's impossible to please the judges in life. And everyone judges you. Eventually everyone eliminates you. How can I check out of this game and still stay involved in life?

What happened to the young Josh who rode Edwards hill on his skateboard back in Zarzamora? There was no competition jersey on me. No sponsor. No judges. No numbers attached to me. No complex and jealous rivals. Just my friend Sam screaming for joy.

And then, randomly, I remember the African church back in Hossegor, where the members talk about God as if he's actually in the room. So does Oma Adri.

She almost never speaks to me in English, but tonight at the campfire, she took my head in her hands and looked me straight in the eye: "Josh, you have what it takes." She gave me an especially intense hug as she left for the evening.

I haven't been able to stay at the fire pit since then and have been wandering around the beach. Some perfect California girl I don't even know is wearing my competition jersey there at the fire pit and partying a little too hard. She's in love with an image of me, but she's barely even met me. I'd rather be disliked for who I am as a person than loved for some projected image of who I am supposed to be.

*

Kati

WHOA. ANOTHER WAVE—up to my waist. The bottom half of my braid is wet now. *Gotta start climbing.* This cliff is all crumbly dirt and sharp rock. Hard to get a footing. *Just…keep…climbing.*

It's hard to see a path to the top. *Wow. What if I don't make it?* My eyes are starting to tear again. *Gotta start over—this way up won't work. No handholds.*

I would love a shot of something strong to drink right now. Jägermeister from Mutti's cabinet? I still have a bit of a beer buzz from earlier. That helps a little with my nerves but fuzzes my concentration.

Mutti sent me off this morning hoping I would meet some stunning California guy at the U.S. Open. There isn't enough money anywhere to pay one of those perfect, confident, tanned guys to invest in me. Which is worse—getting disapproval from Mutti or being ignored by everyone else? Especially men. Except for Zara's cousin, Saahir, not a single man in my life, including my father, ever leans into a conversation with me. It's like I repel all of them.

Mutti hates it when I hang out with Saahir at work. But Zara's dad and her uncle (Saahir's father) schedule us together in their convenience store chain at our request. Saahir and I can talk for hours. But I still try not to look at him when we talk, or I get self-conscious and feel like I'm going to ruin it. We sometimes just get in his car (because of my license issues) and drive together all over LA after work in the middle of the night—the only time to do that without crushing traffic. Talking is easier that way because we both face the same direction.

But that's a dead end too. We're probably too good of friends for him ever to make any kind of move. I would give away all of my sea chest watches if he would reach across the car to my seat, just once, and put his hand on mine, without seeming like he wants to hurry and take it away. If his hand could just touch mine…and stay.

Well, that's not going to happen. Not for me. More burning in my eyes.

There's no one around. What's to stop me from holding onto this especially big rock to my right and sobbing out loud?

Absolutely nothing. So I wail. Literally. Like the Pakistanis at a family funeral. No one can hear me over the pounding of the surf, so I raise my voice and let it rip.

It doesn't help. Nothing gets released. It merely feels like knives in my spirit. So I wail louder. Jewish men would rend their garments in grief. I am slicing my own soul to shreds with each scream.

*

Josh

WHAT'S THAT I SEE at the edge of the water out there? Hard to tell, since it's getting darker. Probably nothing, but something feels disturbed. I'm scanning with total focus as it gets even darker. I can almost feel my pupils dilating all the way open to attract every photon of remaining light.

And, of course, Max and Sam are back at the beach party. Why do they stick by me? All I'll ever be able to do is use my skill to earn points, prize checks, and other useless things. I was a better person four years ago than I am now. What kind of man am I going to become?

Lord, I pray, *anything but my father.*

➤

Kati

LOOKING BACK DOWN OVER MY SHOULDER between primal yells, I see that the water has come up higher on the rocks. Can I even climb down and start over? The incoming tide has blocked my return path. The surf is really loud. It's like standing next to a jet engine. My cheeks are wet with tears, and my legs and braid are wet from the splashing.

I am in deep trouble. I have to reach for that hold up there high and on the right. *Almost. Almost.* Have to commit to get it. A slight little hop…and….no.

No good. Missed. The rest happens like a flash.

A concussion like a baseball bat hits my head, and my left wrist smashes against the rock hard as I spin backward, headfirst into the crashing waves, which sweep me out to sea. I bounce off the sand bottom and push off, the side of my head throbbing and my entire left arm stinging from the salt water.

*

Josh

GOOD LORD, SOMEONE'S OUT THERE in the surf, and she's in trouble. Was that a scream I just heard?

Are you sure, Josh? I ask myself. *Did you really see that? Wait. How do I know it's a she?*

I have a flash of that girl trapped on the Cliffs. Another flash of a girl from long ago on a beach cruiser. I know, without being able to know, that it's a young woman out there.

Yup. Someone is trapped in the impact zone. I have to make a decision in just a few seconds.

*

Kati

I POP THROUGH THE SURFACE in time to see a huge wave about to break right in front of me. It looms up out of the dark. I gasp for air and swim down as hard and fast as I can to try to get under it. Got to get past it and away from the rocks. I open my eyes underwater and strain in the darkish water to see if there is room under the wave turbulence to swim out to safety. Yes, about three feet clearance between the bottom of the underwater rolling half of the wave and the sand.

Swim down deep, Kati, with everything you have. Go girl, go.

*

Josh

I DON'T HAVE A BOARD. No one knows better than I do how dangerous it is out there. Never attempt to save someone unless you yourself have a good chance of surviving. Like a thunderbolt through my soul, I literally shake as I realize that I once put a human being, Max, deliberately into a situation just like that poor victim in the water. What in heaven's name was I thinking? This is my chance to make it right. I may never get another opportunity like this one.

Jogging up to large group of nearby people having a BBQ, their faces lit by their campfire, I spot a huge longboard sticking out of the sand. I dash right through them, getting some sand in their food. I grab the board and scream, "Need this!" and sprint toward the water with the board under my arm.

Where was that flailing hand sticking up out in the surf?

Jesus, O Jesus. Where was it? Why is it that, when we're really in trouble, *Mom* and *Jesus* are the first words that come out of our mouths?

Kati

SOMEHOW I MAKE IT. The wave rumbles right across my back as my knees glance off the sand bottom, and I head back up for air between the waves.

I repeat this three times to get clear of the rocks. It's getting darker. During one breathing break between waves, I check out my left arm. As I hold it out of the water, blood starts to gather and flow down the stinging skin. The Ziffer à Grande Complication 1924 watch is shattered.

Not the watch. No. Not that.

More burning in my throat. Another wave. *Breathe. Dive. Surface. Repeat. Breathe. Dive. Surface. Repeat.*

I shoot a look back at the Cliffs. I can barely see them; they're tiny. I'm caught in a rip current and being whisked out to sea. I feel so helpless. And I'm in the impact zone of relentless waves.

Breathe. Dive. Surface. Repeat.

*

Josh

I RUN INTO THE WATER, splashing as I go. As soon as it gets too deep to run, I thrust myself on top of the board and start paddling straight out.

O Jesus, I'm right. She's in the impact zone without a board. She'll never last out there.

I freeze for a second as I realize that I never had time to fasten my leash to my ankle. If I lose the board, I'll drown for sure. No time to go back and fix the leash right now. It might be too late already. If she goes down for too long in the dark, murky water, I'll never find her.

This is going to be a high-wire act without a net.

And now is all that matters. O Jesus.

*

Kati

I COULDN'T MAKE IT UNDER THE TURBULENCE of the last wave. I got rag-dolled and swallowed a lot of water. I come up, throwing up the salt water as I surface. Frantic, coughing, and also trying just to breathe. I'm headed north and west, along the coast and out to sea at the same time. Useless to fight against the current. And because I'm so skinny, I've never been buoyant. Have to thrash just to keep my face above water.

*

Josh

WHAT AM I DOING OUT HERE? If there is a Creator, and I think there is one, does he notice what I'm doing right now? Does he literally see me, or am I on my own?

Briefly I see Oma Adri. We're standing outdoors on the deck of our Hossegor home at night. Her mother, Nellie, is playing Chopin in the octagonal room right behind her. Oma walks silently toward me and hands me a flaming torch. And then the image evaporates.

*

Kati

I'VE BEEN IN OXYGEN DEBT for what feels like forever. Can't get my heart rate down. *Breathe. Dive. Surface. Repeat.*

The salt water tastes like tears. I could cry this many tears right now. An ocean full. I'm awash in my own infinite grief.

But the tears are going to stop very soon, for good, if I can't get to the beach. Why did I have that last beer? My head isn't clear enough to handle this. *Breathe. Dive. Surface. Repeat.*

*

Josh

I PADDLE THE LONGBOARD FOR ALL I'M WORTH, sprinting right and left to avoid the crests of the oncoming shore-bound waves so perhaps somehow, good Lord willing, I'll make it out to the critical part of the impact zone.

As I compete for my life (at many levels), I realize I have become my father. I make a living off of scoring in sports. My father embodies "resentment" for me, and I am tempted to go back down that well-worn path of blaming him for everything. But a voice that's not a voice says clearly to me, *"Forgive him, Josh, and honor him, and you will be free."*

I burst into tears. From all the pressure of the situation. Out of shame for what I did to Max. Out of horror of the realization that my grievances toward my father are keeping me from being fully alive in this world. By reacting against him, I am unable to act on my own behalf and out of my own heart.

Then love for my father floods into me from a Source I can't identify. I vow right then and there to save this girl, survive, and reconcile with my father. Or die trying.

For whatever reason, as I cross this emotional line with my father, any sense of shame over what I did to Max vanishes all by itself. I'd love to enjoy this moment, but there are two lives on the line, right here and now. I resolve to leave all of my grievances out here in the water and start a new life this evening on the beach.

But for that to happen, I have to make it back to the beach.

*

Kati

THIS IS IT. I can only survive another two or three waves. I wonder if a part of Mutti will be relieved when I don't make it back. Or will this just be my final way of disappointing her?

I shed my wrap dress in one last attempt to increase my chances. Of course the phone is already long gone, but it's not like that matters anymore.

Breathe. Dive. Surface. Repeat.

What would Opa do? He would be calm. He would choose to live. But maybe I should just give up; this is hopeless. I can barely stay alive, let alone swim free of this rip current. The waves are like relentless sideways freight trains, except louder. When they come crashing in, there is nowhere to hide.

My special-needs class at the church flashes before my eyes. I have to, just HAVE to be there for them this coming Sunday. Those families value me without condition. I am changing the lives of their children. If I don't make it back...

Pull yourself together, Kati, I tell myself. *For the kids who love you. Who need you.*

Okay, God, I am yours; save me. Whatever that means, considering the mess I've gotten myself into.

*

Josh

WHERE IS SHE? It's getting too dark. There she is, over to the left, but I can't get there. The wave is crashing down...right on top of her. She's going to get held under. How can I calculate where she'll come up, if she ever does? Can't put myself at risk or we'll both be lost.

A woman's dress, or wrap, or something floats by me in the rushing river of the riptide. Not a good sign.

Focus. Focus. O Jesus. My knees are shaking uncontrollably as a big one rolls in toward me.

*

Kati

AM I HALLUCINATING? I am soaked. But with rain, not salt water. And sitting in a European church, like the one I went to with Opa, but different. There's something bad outside. Very bad. But somehow it hasn't happened yet.

I'm a young man in this vision. That doesn't seem strange, somehow. I'm sitting on the wooden bench, deeply emotional for a reason I can't put my finger on. Everyone else is singing and standing. I'm thinking and feeling in German, but the vision isn't Germany.

A woman's hand, from my left, touches my shoulder....

The vision evaporates.

*

Josh

CAN'T GET AROUND IT. No leash, so I can't ditch the board and dive under the wave. Only one thing to do. I jump off the board and flip it over, fins up, and hang on to the rails. A turtle move—I go underwater and hold tight from underneath. I put all the strength I've ever had into gripping the board as I feel the wave start to roll over me. If the tiny muscles in my fingers fail and I lose my grip on the slick, wet fiberglass, I'll be lost. There will be no way to make it back to shore; the rip current will pull me straight out to sea.

So I'm going to die out here, and no one will ever see it happen. There are thousands of sharks out in the deep channel between here and Catalina Island. No one will even find a trace of my body.

At least I'll be drowned and dead before the razor-sharp teeth rip into me.

*

Kati

BREATHE. DIVE. SURFACE. REPEAT. *God, I am yours. Save me.*

Breathe. Dive. Surface. Repeat. Now would be good, God. Like right now.

Breathe. Dive. Surface. Repeat.

I have enough strength for one more wave. *Now, Lord. NOW.* My throat burns with emotion again, but this time it is pure will to live. To see my kids at church. And Zara. And Saahir.

Yes, Lord. One last breath. Time to dive...

*

Josh

THE THUNDERING WAVE BREAKS over the top of the board and tears and rips at my grip. I am in the spin cycle with no safety net. I am clinging to the fiberglass board for dear life. Turbulent salt water is forced into my ears and mouth against my will.

But my grip holds. I surface and cough as hard as I can to try to clear the salty fluid out of my lungs. I flip the board wax-side up and clamber back up and paddle like mad for the left side of the next peak. She should be coming up for air somewhere. *Focus. Focus.* Where is she?

Now, Jesus! Now! If she doesn't surface right now, it's over for her and doubtful for me.

Her hand bursts through the surface. Right next to me.

In slow motion I see a dramatic tattoo on her right hand. Is this a vision? a dream? No time to think.

*

Kati

A HAND CLAMPS LIKE A VISE onto my right wrist. At first I think it's a shark, but then the most beautiful face I've ever seen is inches from mine.

He speaks. "Hey, I'm Josh. Let's get you back to the beach."

Even in the dark, the blue-white focus of his eyes is simply piercing.

*

Josh

I GRAB HER WRIST and throw her, belly down, across the top of the longboard. She is so skinny and light that it's easy to do.

I plop down on top of her and paddle for my life. And hers.

*

Kati

HE QUICKLY PIVOTS THE BOARD toward shore, lines me up on the waxy, sticky deck on my stomach, slaps his body right down on top of my skinny frame (which almost knocks the wind out of me), and paddles like a madman. His head is right behind mine.

I put my face down into the wax on the nose of the board, not bearing to watch. The wave comes behind us and lifts the tail of the board high. With three heavy strokes, Josh starts to catch the wave. We shoot forward like a rocket as the massive wave picks us up and rifles us at an angle along its face toward the beach.

We are skimming across the water so fast that I can hardly open my eyes because of the spray.

Josh screams a primal victory shout: "Maaaaaais oooouuuuiiiii!" right in my ears.

I'm laughing, breathing, crying, sobbing. He carves long,

swooping left and right turns with the board, seemingly just for fun.

Elation...life. I'm going to see the kids on Sunday. Zara. Saahir. His mother in the kitchen. I'm going to live.

More tears. Where do they keep coming from?

We hit the sand in what feels like only a few seconds. We roll off the board into the shallow surf.

His friends are running toward us, bringing beach towels. Fist-bumps all around. I black out as they wrap me up....

I come to sitting in a folding chair, wrapped still in towels, in front of a beach fire. The guys, including Josh, are playing touch football on the sand in the dark near a parking lot streetlamp. They're close by, but a little too far away to yell for them with all the wind. We apparently are at Bolsa Chica Beach, north of the Cliffs.

My head is throbbing; my arm is scraped. The priceless Ziffer watch is ruined, so I have no idea what time it is. I take it off and place it on the concrete fire ring. I grab a piece of charcoal and write *Thanks, Josh* on the concrete next to the watch. He'll never know just how thankful I really am, but it's the only thing I can do. There's no way I could explain to him that, in the last hour, for the first time in my life, my world has shifted into balance...as if I've been walking tilted, and now I'm standing straight.

All I have on is a swimsuit, so I keep one of the huge beach towels (is that stealing?) wrapped around me. I turn and slip through a break in the wild blackberry bush along the path, stepping into the dark through what appears to be a broken concrete wall.

I have a long way to go tonight to find Zara, and I don't have time for drama with these guys.

I have a life to live.

2031
Melrose District
Los Angeles, California

Parents have been bringing children in for the last half hour to a room filled with large, colorful, plastic toys.

Kati enters the door, almost as lean as when we saw her last, carrying a largish pile of work stuff while checking her hand screen. Her thick, barely tamed, incredibly long braid now has a touch of gray weaving through it. Since her hair is pulled back into the braid, her gold nose stud adds even more emphasis to her most prominent facial feature. Her summer dress sports the latest of colors—just on the borderline of being too trendy for someone over forty.

She still loves to bike along the shops on Melrose and "shake the bushes" going through the racks. She wears one of the fabulously expensive sea chest Swiss men's watches on her left wrist; today it's the IWC. We catch a glimpse of the ThornHeart tattoo on her other wrist as she shifts the pile in her arms.

"Mama Kati!" the children shout, and giggles break out.

Kati is in charge here.

She has been married to Zara's cousin, Saahir, for a long time. They have five children of their own. The oldest ones attend Bancroft School and will go through confirmation at Hope Lutheran during the next two years.

She is in and out all during the week, having secured a team of major donors (and, of course, her share of the Krugerrands from the sea chest) to fund her little school, which is free to all students. Her work as a special-needs Sunday school volunteer at the church led in a straight line to this vocation, over time. This is a school for children diagnosed with Down syndrome.

Laying the stack of work on the counter-ledge by the office, Kati says hello to the receptionist and then walks through the room, greeting the children one by one with her high-beam smile and a light touch on the cheek. Young ones and older ones. A handful are larger than she is. But all clearly adore Mama Kati.

As she glides and "dances" through the room, it's clear that her seemingly inborn awkwardness has been lifted out of her. She is the central hub of this little universe of unconditional love and acceptance that she has created.

On the left wall a bold mural painted in bright colors is titled Psalm 89:2. The Hebrew-lettered words *Chesed, Amen, Olam, Shamayim* splash about the wall. "Everlasting Love," "Solid Support," "Big and Boundless," "Water-colored Sky" are the meanings to those Middle Eastern Bible concepts that float around in the core of human dreaming and vision.

Painted swirls of water burst out of the sky and through a broken stone wall. The mural sings silently somehow. You can hear it with your spirit. The mural is signed at the bottom:

Happy 40th, Kati!
—Zara

Kati often hums songs from Sunday worship during the week; it's as if she's always about to break into song. The gospel choir at Hope

Lutheran has developed new forms of spontaneous singing, which are attracting attention from all around the Los Angeles area. The new songs are composed right in the moment, based on the prayers of the people present that day, collected earlier, and no one really knows where they will end up. A growing contingent of local neighborhood Orthodox Jews is showing up at Hope to experience this, and one of them is teaching a course at the church on the Hebrew concepts in the psalms (which inspired the mural). The pastor forbids recording of this singing, believing that its "present" nature is sacred, and that to replay it would miss the point.

Kati floats over to the door on our right and pulls down her apron and goggles from a hook, calling out, "Shop time!"

The older children hurry to join her (and we follow along before the door closes) into the shop in the next room. It is filled with tools. Even as tool time with Opa was therapy for Kati, she now guides the children through the art of crafting as a means to unlocking new connections in their minds. Only a handful at a time ever come with her into the shop—she likes to spend time with each student, and, of course, make sure they are all safe.

A framed portrait of Opa hangs on the wall above the main workbench. Many of the tools are from his workshop in Germany, which Kati had shipped over.

She has achieved remarkable results with the children, reaching levels of dexterity and skill thought unattainable for Down syndrome kids.

It has been a long time since that day on the beach, yet Kati will always remember....

2031
Melrose District
Los Angeles, California

Kati

IT DIDN'T GO WELL, a couple of decades ago, when I told Mutti I wasn't going to attend USC after all, and a few years later, that I was dating a Pakistani. Both of us made a lot of threats...none of which were carried out, thank God. Saahir talked to my parents one night when I was at Zara's a few months after the rescue, and that helped some. Guess it's hard to argue with someone like Saahir, because he's so straight up, reasonable, and friendly.

I don't think Mutti and I will ever be on the same wavelength... and Dad? He still doesn't figure much in my world. Our relationship will never be easy, but at least now we three can coexist on the planet without as much stress.

As for dating Saahir, it was so clear he was headed somewhere in life, and I wanted to go that somewhere with him. Saahir is physically unremarkable. No woman would be drawn to a picture of him. But I was always attracted to his brightness and energy. He seems to know what to do, without any hesitation, and I love being around that. Even better, he loves me for *me*...even when I was invisible to everyone else. It just took me years to notice his interest.

As for the career I chose, well, it sort of happened. As a girl, I was always disappointed when the weekly church sessions with the special-needs kids ended. Some of my happiest teen memories were from church—when the kids in my class would run and cling to my legs. I was so starving for human touch, I'd simply melt at the beginning of each Sunday class.

So when I got older, I kept working with special-needs kids. Slowly, it grew into a regular class, and then a school. My second-oldest, our son, volunteers there now. It's as if Opa skipped a generation and reappeared in young Ebrahim.

The kids in my class embody for me a key Hebrew concept from the Psalms: *Chesed,* pronounced "KHEH-sud." It means God's unconditional and unearned love for everyone on earth. I unconditionally love and accept my students, and they do the same for me, as both teacher and friend. (You see, Opa Harald's legacy still does live on—in me and in my students.)

As I look around the workshop here at the school, I also see the movie posters for the stage sets I've worked on. Some of the films were embarrassingly bad, but the sets were good! I still hang out at the studio and plan on doing at least two or three more major projects at some point.

That night at the Cliffs awakened a voice inside me. It was the same voice I first started to hear while leaning on Opa's shoulder, listening to the organist in Germany. The more I listened to the voice—so still and small that you can miss it—the more my awkwardness went away and I started to feel peaceful. I haven't been chronically agitated in years.

The voice would start to sing when I was with Saahir at the store or driving around LA with him, when I was in church with the special-needs kids, when I thought about having a child, and then more children. The voice helped me embrace my incurable skinniness and my rather remarkable nose. The voice would sing calmness into me when Mutti raged against my "foolish" decisions.

The more the voice sang, the less I needed to steal alcohol and binge drink from my parents' cabinet. By the time I married Saahir, who was raised as an alcohol-free Muslim, I rarely drank—although I still enjoy sneaking a glass of primo Justin Isosceles wine with Zara once in a while. It was within the verses of that inner song that I stopped lying to my parents and started implementing the vision for the special-needs school.

Now the voice sings when the woodchips fly on my latest project, and when I put on one of Walter's sea chest watches.

That day at the Cliffs re-indexed my whole life and emotional orientation. Now I get up in the morning and feel joy. I no longer index my decisions around pleasing people and meeting impossible expectations. I decide based on an audience of one—the *Shekinah* voice, as my Orthodox Jewish girlfriends in the neighborhood say.

I still haven't cut my hair, but I no longer wear it long to spite Mutti. Like reading the rings of a redwood trunk, each twist in my long braid merely reminds me of the path I've taken—the long and winding journey that brought me here, to this moment. Also, Saahir's mother, a traditional Pakistani with hair as long as mine, loves to comb it out for me and rebraid it. She says often, "Long hair, long life!" in her singsong Urdu accent.

She also—at first with hesitation, thinking I would ignore or reject it—gave me her mother's heirloom gold nose stud, which I first wore at our wedding, a gift that had been handed down through her family for generations. She wept when I agreed to pierce my nose and wear it for the rest of my life. It was also a deliberate action, on my part, to affirm my nose and my appearance—that central feature of my face I used to see as my ugliest feature. I now love the way God made me.

When I pass on, I'll leave it for one of my granddaughters. I also wore a traditional Pakistani wedding dress with flamboyant colors. As you can imagine, Mutti was not pleased. But I've learned to love her without having to meet her expectations. We've actually begun to get along. I so regret being angry with her as a teen. I now see that my resentment of her expectations was just as ensnaring as the expectations themselves.

It's been quite a process for her too. It's good that Saahir and I are very prosperous. It helps her look past the eccentric braid, fedoras, tattoo, men's watches, and nose stud. Bless her heart. And I think my children like her better than they like me—that seems to run in the family. Yet the kids help me see all the good in her that I was blind to at their age.

I've started to repeat Mutti's fave Dutch phrase: "*Doe normal, dan doe je al gek genoeg* (Act normal, and then you'll already act crazy enough)."

A few years after the Cliffs, I started to see that all the beautiful things that Opa had said about me were true. But not in a comparative way. No one is more beautiful than anyone else. I am not special, and neither are you. You see, *special* always carries comparative baggage. I learned this from working with the kids at church. Every human is infinitely and equally valuable. We don't raise that value by achieving more than others. Our Creator creates us equal.

I don't work with these children because I'm better than these "needy" kids and want to "help" them with my superiority. Instead, I create a loving community with them to celebrate our equality and shared human fellowship. I level the playing field so we can unlock our gifts together. Whenever I see sweet little Roberta's cherubic smile, Jamie happily clapping out of rhythm to music, or remember the day five-year-old Marcus spoke his first words, my cup of joy and thankfulness overflows. Then I celebrate, once again, the day at the Cliffs, where my life took a completely different path.

I know now, without doubt, that we were all put on this earth for a reason, and sometimes it's the subtle little things—the seemingly random, chance encounters—that lead to huge breakthroughs that lead us to discover this.

I'm convinced that our "goodness" (my church friends call it "holiness") comes not from effort but by yielding to this infinite love and goodness that God keeps piling up for us. It's not about effort and discipline but rather about opening ourselves up to all that God has for us. And listening to the ongoing singing of the *Shekinah* voice.

Faith is a process, I've discovered. I don't have everything figured out—far from it. But I find comfort in the fact that the Jesus I've come to know was not perfect because he was gifted at meeting complex expectations. He was perfect because he followed the voice of God, because he did what his Father asked him to do.

That same passion is what has led me to where I am today.

And I love my life.

~ BEHIND THE STORY ~
Angelo

A teen girl's voice wakes Kati from her daydream musings. Looking up from her project, the teenager beckons Kati over with both of her hands straight in the air. Her name is Rose, and she has been working on her chessboard for a year and a half. Rose has been spontaneously elated by its developing beauty and wants to share the moment with Kati.

As Kati approaches her, Rose runs her fingers once more across the beautifully oiled wooden chessboard squares. She reaches up and takes Kati's head with both hands, kisses her on the forehead, exactly on the spot where Opa used to kiss her, and then young Rose lets out an uninhibited cheer and claps with glee.

Kati touches her own just-kissed forehead with her tattooed hand and drinks in the unearned love shown by Rose. Love flowing straight from God. Piling up faster than she can ever use it.

Standing, Kati walks past a full-length mirror on the way back to the tool bench. A tall, lean, quirky-looking woman with a sparkle in her eye looks back at her. Kati brushes a couple of stray hairs away from her forehead and pauses for an unrushed look at herself from top to bottom. She flashes herself her high-beam smile and loves what she sees.

The intercom bell rings, and the receptionist calls out, "Kati, package for you in the office."

Kati couldn't be more surprised by the contents of the package, or the note that accompanied it:

Dear Katarina,

I would like to think that I saved your life, but I sometimes doubt that it actually happened. I don't mean this romantically, but literally—you are the girl of my dreams. I'll explain later. My wife, Lindsey, and I would love to meet you. I believe that this watch is yours. My contact info is on the printed chip under my signature.

Josh

Katarina holds the shattered Ziffer à Grande Complication 1924 in her tattooed right hand, undoes the IWC, and slowly buckles Walter's broken Ziffer onto her left wrist.

Rechecking the note, she sees a red-ink stamp of the Dornbusch family shield at the bottom by the signature. That simply can't be. But it is. She puts on her fedora and leaves immediately, hoping to find Josh within a few hours.

Her backstory is about to light up, this very day, in ways she can't imagine....

*

2031
Zarzamora, California

Josh

HOW COULD SOMETHING that big and heavy be missing?
I've looked all over the house and workshop for it.

Occasionally I get promptings to do things that I don't fully understand. A few months ago, while doodling my millionth edition of the ThornHeart on some paper during a staff meeting, I got the urge to recreate the design in iron. And so I did.

I might have ignored this prompting save for the markings on that girl's wrist I grabbed in the water off the Cliffs some two decades ago.

The tattoo on her hand was exactly the same as the design from my dreams and from the rubber stamp I had made when I was a kid. The same one I doodle over and over. Year in and year out.

Because of the drama of that day, we parted in the dark before I remembered to ask her about the origin of her tattoo. I hope I'll get the chance to do so someday.

I've often wondered what happened to that skinny girl with the long braid and why she was out there on the Cliffs in the first place. Right about today, she should be getting a package from me. A couple of weeks ago, I ran across the smashed watch—not something I would normally keep, but it's the only thing I have to remember that girl by and that very strange day that changed everything in my life. My dear bride, Lindsey, recently encouraged me to look for her; nowadays you can find anyone on Search. She said it would be good for me to ensure that the rescue really happened—memory can be a funny thing.

The still-skinny woman often talks to me in my dreams. I am trying to picture her expression when she sees the watch.... Somehow I have a feeling she'll be calling this week. Funny, she has a Pakistani name; there must be a story behind that, since the girl I saw in the water clearly wasn't Asian. But doesn't every event have a story behind it?

The rescue back at the Cliffs was so cleansing. My growing

agitation evaporated that night…and it's never returned. It's as if I started seeing with a clear focus for the first time ever, and I knew what I had to do. Where I had to go. Who I had to be.

No more trying to meet everybody's expectations. No more trying to hide who I really was.

When I returned from rescuing the girl that day, I was a different person. Oma Adri knew. She cocked her head toward me and then listened…as if hearing a distant voice. I'll never forget her smile—tentative at first, questioning. And then she opened her arms to welcome me in. She repeated, "Josh, you have what it takes."

We've had so much snow this winter. An old-school snowboarder like myself can't complain about all the fresh powder. I'm just back from a workday as the director of the Gold Mine Snow Resort. Honestly, the owners only pay me for my presence there. I'm basically a celebrity human advertisement and a goodwill ambassador. Business has improved since I started there, and they pay me well.

I'm sitting in my recliner looking around at what passes for a study. The drawing board. The mementos and awards from the longest-running TV show of our generation: *JoshGlobal*. A photo of me in the Himalayas. Me at Mammoth. Me with Bear Grylls in Africa. Me at Teahupoo. Me at Jordy Smith's retirement. Tony Hawk and Kelly Slater having dinner at our house here. Me dropping in at Pipe. My show was a celebration of all that is *steezy* and *mooi* in action sports. No competition. No scores. Stunning photography. Lots of travel and digging into the hearts of those who, figuratively speaking, can hold on to that weightless cartwheel feeling just for the joy of it.

In my hand is the rubber stamp I had made so many years ago. I push hard onto the semidry red inkpad and print ThornHearts on the paper next to my chair.

Then I'm back at searching for what's missing—the iron

version of the ThornHeart, about the size of a Frisbee, which I forged and crafted in my shop/studio out back. It has to be in the house somewhere! Lindsey says she heard someone in the house last night, but by the time I got up and looked around, brandishing the Ethiopian sword I keep under the bed, there was only the sound of Oma Adri snoring. Nothing else was missing, so it could not have been a burglar. The back door was closed but unlocked. But that's pretty common in this small town—we don't lock things much around here. I couldn't remember if I had locked it or not before going to bed.

We live right on Water Street, the first house after the last business, which is an abandoned phone company building that has been turned into one of the new coffee libraries. We grow our own vegetables and spices in the spacious garden a few blocks away behind the old broken-down stone wall ruins. Our six children sleep in the two big bunkhouses I built out back. A generation ago, people had such small families; glad that's starting to change.

The old Methodist building where I used to go with my mom is now a combined school, church, and social club. We are there at least a few evenings a week, having a lot of meals together with the other families. Our kids go to school there, and we often join them for the evenings, walking home together afterward before bed.

In a few years, our oldest daughter, Nellie, will finish school and head south of the border for her national service obligation. She gets to choose the country, and she's loved Costa Rica ever since our family surfing vacations there, and during filming sessions, when she was younger. It's a direct train ride to Costa Rica from the station in Santa Barbara, and since the energy revolution, train travel has been free all over the Western Hemisphere. A lot of retired couples seem never to get off the trains.

Dad is back in insurance work in Holland. He's also joined an athletic club, where he volunteers with young people. Letting go of all my grievances against him has allowed me to enjoy him for who he is. Some of my best recent memories are of him traveling with our crew as we filmed *JoshGlobal* on location all over the world. Mom was never into extreme "feral" travel, so she didn't join us on trips much.

Every time I think about the iron ThornHeart or search in vain for it, the same words come to me: *"Thanks—it's for Nellie."* I even promised God I was going to give it to my daughter if I could ever locate it again, but what would a teenage girl do with something like that? No one would steal it—it would be worth very little at a flea market. And how could it be for my great-grandmother Cornelia/Nellie, who has been dead for years?

Something tells me I'm not going to see it again.

I get more and more words that just come to me from somewhere as I get older. I was raised in a time when that seemed to happen to people less often. The Global South has taught us in the less spiritual North how to listen with our spirits.

Last summer, when Gemechis was here from Ethiopia (the one who gifted me with that sword under my bed), he taught for a full week of evenings about how better to listen to the Spirit. The meeting room has hardwood floors and glass Palladian windows that seem to let in more sunlight than there actually is. We sat in a circle on surprisingly comfortable Shaker-style chairs for the teachings. Gemechis did a series on "My Sheep Hear My Voice" and shared his boyhood experiences listening to God in the Mekane Yesus Church in Africa.

After he was done, Lindsey stood up and prayed for openness, and all of us there were flooded with inaudible words that seemed to come from the same Source. We talked about it among ourselves for days.

The moon is out now, and Lindsey is calling from down the hall to take a walk with her in the snow. I close the inkpad and leave our home with her, heading down the alley, our steps crunchy in the snow, to the trail that leads to the abandoned orchard. As we climb through the rubble of the broken-down wall, I am grateful for those little things in life that make all the difference.

My thoughts turn to the chess set that Oma Adri bought for me so long ago. You see, life is a stalemate. At some point, you have to step out of the game into a new way of living. Only by abandoning all attempts to meet others' expectations can you truly hear the voice of the Spirit and be freed to pursue what God would have you uniquely do.

As I help Lindsey over the last knee-high stone, slippery from the ice, I remember my parents' story about the day I was born—the day the Berlin Wall fell. I wonder what happened to all the other babies born on that day. We share a lot with people who live in the same exact time period as we do—we experience the same slice of the world's story. Somehow, within all this, destiny is fixed and freedom is real. Don't ask me how the two fit together, but they do. And the pivot points in our life story are tiny shifts that lead us to a whole new future.

So tonight as we walk, Lindsey and I laugh together about the missing iron artwork. We reminisce about our travels during the shooting of *JoshGlobal*. We marvel at how bright winter nights can be with a full moon and snow cover. We joke about how bad clothing used to be—how we used to get cold on evenings like this one. Remember how bulky winter wear was a couple of decades ago? My kids love to laugh at pictures of me in my old snowboard gear.

I'm getting a lucid vision, as I look up at the moon through the stark, bare branches of the orchard, of a European churchyard. Organ music is playing. In the center is an old iron gate. Why do I avoid looking at the gate?

Somehow I know that it's time for something to be "made right."
I squeeze Lindsey's gloved hand and wipe a little tear from my eye
with my other hand.

A word-phrase that Jesus spoke on the cross comes to me in the
original Greek: *tetelesthai.* It is finished.

My hand screen vibrates. The text message rotates into place:

Josh & Lindsey: In Ur driveway. U in town?
—Katarina & Saahir

2031
Hillegersberg, Holland

Come with me again to the Hillegonda Church on the little graveyard mound in Hillegersberg on this sunny day. I have a surprise for you. Have you guessed what it is?

For the second time in this story (and everything is a story), I am going to intervene in the physical world, which overlaps with the world of dreams and the world of visions and truth. Your instincts may want to label me as an angel, but that label carries so much baggage in your world.

I'm not a Precious Moments figurine, and I don't have wings. A lot of you also believe that people become angels when they die, but angels are angels and people are people. When I appear, people tend to be afraid, which is why we always have to greet them with...well...

Enough of that. To the task at hand!

You can probably guess what I am carrying up the crunchy sounding gravel path to the church. The dinner-plate-sized iron ring is cold in my hands but warm and good at a heart level. I feel its rightness running up my arms. Perhaps Josh will (with quite a shock) discover his artwork here someday. But that's, as they say, another story.

In fact, have you ever noticed that things just disappear from your possession and you can't find them? If so, perhaps they are being put to use somewhere by one of us…?

I'm doing this for Nellie.

The cosmic checkbook must be balanced. Cornelia, Nellie, passed on in an elite retirement home in Ommoord many years ago, her hair, as always, neatly combed over her scars. She's never, for obvious reasons, been back to this place, so I am standing in for her.

We hear an organist, whom we cannot see from here, practicing in the church as we approach the dreaded gate. Bach. "*O Haupt voll Blut und Wunden*"[*] comes wafting into the sunlit graveyard through the wide-open windows, on this unusually warm winter morning just after sunrise.

The generational family blessing has come full circle. Some people in the story worked with us; some ignored us. Sometimes *you* work with us; sometimes *you* ignore us.

But faith and blessing will always find a way to be fruitful and multiply. The faith of Nellie and Walter, imperfect as they were, had a certain power and grace to it that lived on through Adri, Harald, and Janine. And, of course, it flowered again with Josh and Kati. Faith, like water, will always find its way back to its Source. Carry it, and it will carry you. Receive it from others, and pass it on to them.

Until this sunny morning, the blackberry bush where you and I did our hiding back in the 1940s has grown, untrimmed, to the point where it has virtually engulfed the iron grating in its thorny clutches. That is about to change, and you won't believe your eyes. Just watch.

As I lift the metal ThornHeart chest high in front of me, just yards from the gate, the iron artwork in my hands starts to glow. The glow begins to repel the blackberry branches, and they literally retreat around behind the now-bared, rusty, black-iron gate.

---

[*] "O Sacred Head Now Wounded"

You can hear the rustling and snapping as I approach, step by step, and the gnarled vines shrink away. I notice that a wooden board with barely visible writing on it is lodged in the base of the vine stems: VERRADER (traitor).

As I place the ThornHeart on the gate, it vibrates and glows even brighter, melting onto the iron bars in a weld that will never be broken. I let go, and it cools into its permanent place. Rust from all around me falls as powdered orange dust to the ground from the decades-old gate and fence. A fresh, shiny coat of black paint seeps out from inside the iron itself. It dries instantly in the first light of the sunrise. Incredible, but not surprising, somehow.

Restoration. I scan the base of the blackberry bush for the VERRADER sign. Gone. Way gone. I smile.

It takes a crown of thorns and a truly good heart to destroy the wounding thorns of life.

The organist finishes the Bach piece, as if waiting on me. Organ music always hangs in the air for a couple of seconds after the hands leave the keys. I breathe deeply and let my emotions flow out like the receding tide to the point where I am once again able to speak. I brush some powdered rust off of my black sleeves and take a step back. I stand formally at attention.

I whisper, "For Nellie," and everything around me shifts back to the way it should be. A cosmic fever seems to break, and we are able to breathe with more ease in this place. Curses are meant to be broken.

If you pay attention with your spirit, you will notice these kind of shifts. They happen all the time. Evil and brokenness are never even any good at being evil and broken. The pharaoh always ends up at the bottom of the Red Sea. The evil dictator must die by suicide. Good is simply good at being good. And prevailing.

If you remember right, I only intervened in the physical realm one other time in this story—to save baby Adri from the mob that was coming for Nellie. When we pick up the story of Adri another time, you'll see why this was so terribly necessary.

For now, I touch the cooled metal heart and trace the crown of thorns with the tips of my left fingers. This kind of place is one of those Centers around which everything moves and out of which everything is created—the sort of place where pain, blood, and redemption cross paths to meet. And keep meeting. And will always meet. If you're in a hurry to finish the story, you might want to stop and reread this paragraph before moving on. I guarantee it'll be worth your while.

If anyone or anything tries to curse or kill the Goodness in the Center of all things, it will just keep coming back to life. Forever Easter. For Nellie. For you. True Goodness is unsinkable.

And once you've been to this Center, this Truth, you'll know your way everywhere. You are never lost again.

Twice, then. We intervened twice in this story. So far.

Let me tell you a secret. If you are old enough to read this book, we have intervened in your life at least twice. Your story makes no sense without this fact.

And we will intervene again.

And again.

And something you have might go missing and appear somewhere else where it is needed.

Come and awaken to this Truth.

And never, ever go back to sleep.

TAKING IT DEEPER

ABOUT THE BOOK

The Blackberry Bush is basically a story about Josh and Kati, both born the day the Berlin Wall falls in 1989, and their coming of age and understanding.

As with all births, there is a big backstory, reaching to the generation of their great-grandparents struggling through the Second World War. We are all products of an extensive root system, whether we believe it or acknowledge it.

Both Kati and Josh have Dutch and German heritage. Both spend time living in California and along the Rhine River in Europe.

Kati spends her first decade in Europe; Josh in California. Then, seemingly randomly, they swap places around the time of the World Trade Center attacks.

Kati struggles with the dark side of disapproval from others. Josh struggles with the dark side of talent and competition. Their broken responses to impossible demands ensnare them in the all-too-common human condition of self-entrapment. They find themselves in need of rescue.

They also awaken to locating their place in the relational "Olympic torch relay" of generational blessings in a season of waning spirituality in the Western World.

Guided especially by wise grandparents, they begin to unpack, over the years, both their heritage and their destiny, their roots and their wings.

Euclid, the Greek geometer, taught us ages ago that perfectly parallel lines never meet. Since Josh's and Kati's lines are not perfectly parallel, they do meet…for a brief moment. And that seemingly random moment (ah, but if you've read the book you now know that is not so) is what changes the trajectory of each of their lives forever.

QUESTIONS
FOR DISCUSSION

*Great to work through alone; best in a group,
book club, or classroom setting*

Level One

1. Josh loved Adri, and Kati loved Harald—their grandparents.
What is/was your relationship with your grandparents like? With
which older person have you been the closest in life? Why were you
attracted to that person?

2. If this story was a movie and you were in charge of casting,
whom would you choose to play the different characters? Explain.

3. Who do you believe the narrator was? Have you ever had an encounter with someone where an "angel option" is the best explanation? Share the story.

4. Josh has skills and abilities that set him apart from others. Has that ever been painful for you? Have you ever hidden a gift because it would make others uncomfortable? If so, tell what happened. Why do some people—especially teens—"dumb down" to become more popular? What does it cost them in the long run?

5. If you have a best friend, what is the biggest tension between the two of you? Kati struggled with jealousy with Zara. Joshua's competition with Max turned ugly. How do you handle the tensions in your relationship?

6. See how many times you can find the imagery of the blackberry bush in the story. What does the "blackberry bush" mean to you?

7. Which character in the novel would you love to spend more time with? Why?

8. Nellie was tarred and feathered for fraternizing with the occupying German enemy army. Why do you think the punishments for treason were so severe?

9. If you were a citizen of an occupying country and it looked as though that invading country would win, how would you respond? Would you consider—for the good of your family perhaps—collaborating with the occupying military? Would you just keep your head down and hope no one notices you? Or would you resist against the invading army? Explain.

10. Josh had a favorite painting. Do you? If so, what is it, and why do you love it? How does it "speak" to you?

11. Kati struggled most of her life with the way she looks. What, do you think, leads to the fact that growing girls, especially, deal with so much body image pressure? If you are a girl/woman, how do you handle it?

12. Josh avoids organized sports while growing up. What are some of the good things and bad things about youth sports? Can they be overdone? What experience(s) have you or those you know had to back your thoughts?

13. Josh continued to doodle the ThornHeart and octagons for years on end. Are there patterns that you sketch over and over? If so, describe them. Why do they have a hold on you?

14. How much pressure have you felt from your parents to achieve their dreams for you? How much of it is real and how much is in your mind?

15. Josh's and Kati's future lives in 2031 are a little different than the world we live in. What do you think will be better in the next generation? What do you think will be worse? What one thing would you change about the way young people grow up, in order to make the world a better place?

16. If you were to write a sequel to this book, what characters would you include? What would the story line be?

Level Two

1. Josh and Kati were born in very dramatic historical times of great change. What are the special challenges of the generation born around 1990? What are their special advantages?

    Is this your generation? If so, what does the rest of the population misunderstand about your age-group?

2. Linda and Konrad in Germany, and Janine and Michael in California were giving birth when the Wall came down in 1989. Where were you when the Berlin Wall fell (if you were alive at the time)?

    Are you familiar with the geography of Cold War Europe? Have you heard the term *Iron Curtain*? If so, what does it mean to you? How would life have differed on each side of the Wall?

3. Kati and Josh struggle with finding freedom in their lives. Do you believe in predestination? Are there multiple possible futures or only one? If there is a God who knows the future, can there really be more than one possible future?

What do the following words mean to you: *fate, destiny, determinism*?

4. Where were you during the World Trade Center attack (if you were alive at the time)? What do you remember thinking and feeling? What two or three things have changed for everyone since then? Have we, as a society, regained our balance since then? Why or why not?

5. Josh loved to skateboard, surf, and snowboard. How much of this do you think was a reaction against his father's more conventional sports life, and how much was genuinely because he loved those sports? Why is it hard to tell where our preferences come from for doing what we do?

6. Kati and Josh were raised going to church. What are the upsides and downsides of such a childhood? Why do you think this seems to be declining in the Western world? Is that good or bad for society?

7. Kati and Josh both attended some lively churches. What is the most interesting church you've attended (if you've been to one)? Why? What makes the difference between a church that is "alive" and one that is "dead"? What one thing could a church change to make you want to come back?

8. Josh develops his ability to be present in "lucid" dreams while he is asleep. Are you aware that you are dreaming while it's happening? Explain, using your own experience.

9. Nellie faces hatred and brutality at the tar-and-feather incident. For those of you who have never experienced such an event, is it hard to believe that these things really happen? Do you think all human beings possess the potential for brutality given the right conditions? Why or why not? Could you picture yourself becoming part of a mob like the one that attacked Nellie? Explain.

10. Kati struggled with alcohol abuse. Why do you think church people have a hard time talking about alcohol? Many of them just edit all references to it out of their language. Since Jesus made copious amounts of wine at the wedding in Cana, why do his followers today have such a fixation on alcohol as a negative thing? If you are in a church, how do you handle discussions of alcohol as a group?

11. Do you speak other languages? Do you have extended family members who have first languages other than English? Do you think more people will become at least bilingual in the future? Why or why not?

12. Zarzamora is the one fictional city in the novel. It's in California. Look up the literary roots for California's name. California is the world center for media and popular storytelling. Do you think this has been a good thing or a bad thing for the world? Explain.

13. Walter and Nellie defied family, morals, and national ethics— but good eventually came from their poor choices. What's the best thing you've seen come out of something that started out wrong? Tell the story.

14. Both Nellie and Josh crossed the line and deliberately chose to do something that most of us would consider wrong. It was not just a mistake in either case. Are you comfortable talking to others about deliberate ethical "felonies" you've committed, or do you keep such things to yourself? Why?

15. Kati faced drowning at the Cliffs. What's the closest you've come to death? Did you bargain with God? Tell the story.

16. In the epilogue, both Josh and Kati have large families of their own, but they come from family lines with very few children. Do you think families can get too small? Would children be better adjusted, in general, with more siblings or with fewer? Explain your reasoning.

17. How have your parents' dreams for you influenced you for the good and for the bad throughout your life thus far? If you are an adult, how has your relationship with your parents changed since your growing-up days?

18. Kati's volunteering with the kids at the church led to her adult vocation. When have you seen your own—or anyone else's—avocation turn into a career?

19. This book has a lot of Christian content. Does that make it, in your mind, a "Christian book"? Or is it just literature with Christian themes? Would you recommend it to your local high school for an English class reading list? Why or why not? Do you think we can have books with spiritual content in the public marketplace, or do they have to be "sanitized"? Explain.

20. Kati's Opa Harald states that we "are in the presence of a God who speaks." Have you ever received a message, in any form, that you believe was from God? How do you think God prefers communicating with us?

21. Has a minor event in your life ever led to a whole new destiny? If so, share the story.

22. Saahir calls Jesus "Isa." Are there different names out there for the same God, or do different names denote totally different realities? Can any faith system claim to be exclusively genuine? Is it really possible to say that all faith systems are the same?

23. For Josh and Kati, their faith came alive as the story went on. What do you think it means to be "saved," and when do you think each of them, if you believe they did, crossed that line? Is salvation a process or an event? Is it possible to say yes to a lot of truths about God without being "saved"?

24. Which of your ancestors was carrying a torch of faith for the family? Was it passed on to you, or do you have to light your own? Explain.

25. Of everyone in your sphere of influence—family, friends, coworkers, and neighbors—which one person would benefit most from reading this story? Why do you think that?

Then pass it along!

For more interaction, follow the author on
Twitter @RobinwoodChurch

INTERVIEW WITH THE AUTHOR

Is this book autobiographical?

No. I identify with a tiny piece of each of the characters and occasionally am repelled by them. I came up with the thirteen main characters before writing the plot and developed them in great detail before letting them interact with each other. Some have taken on a life of their own and started doing things in the book I didn't like. Adi intimidates me, so I didn't give her much airtime in this book. That will come in a later volume. All this being said and getting back to the question, everything in every novel comes out of the author's head.

You seem very familiar with the geography. What's with that?

I absolutely love the region from Oberwinter to Rotterdam along the Rhine shipping lanes; it's a second homeland for me. I was a Fulbright Scholar at the University of Bonn, and I know Ommoord well. My wife and I lived in Oberwinter for a year and deeply appreciated the church there; Wendy sang in the choir. If you look carefully, I put the two of us in a cameo....

I make my real home in Huntington Beach, California, where I walk to the pier (or drive to the Cliffs) and surf most days. My imaginary home in California, of course, is in Zarzamora. In California, you see, we have both—there is a fine line between fantasy and reality here.

Why all the symbolism around blackberry bushes?

1. They start out pleasurable but start to take over. Just like the darker parts of human behavior.
2. They can draw blood.
3. Over time, the combination of impossible demands (from parents, God, society, peers, etc.) and our broken responses to these demands creates a thorny thicket from which we cannot free ourselves. This bramble separates us from our Maker.
4. Freedom from the blackberry bush requires a total shift in orientation to a more spiritual mode that is less indexed on meeting the demands of others.

There is much, much more, if you think about it for a while. But this should get you started on your own musings.

Your inside views of the churches are more spiritual than theological in this novel. What camp are you in?

I avoid theological labels and -isms. But I am drawn to churches that are uninhibited in their worship of God, especially churches with roots in the Global South. The churches in Hossegor and Zarzamora are fictional, but all embody this ideal. The warehouse church in Ommoord is loosely based on the Evangelische Gemeente on Bertrand Russell Street. Delightful people. Visit them on a Sunday. Robinwood Church, my home church in California, which meets in a warehouse, has this vibe.

My theology is conservative, but I don't think God is all that impressed with anyone's theology, including mine. I just want to know and love God and do the same with people. Jesus taught me that.

What motivated you to write this book?

I've always had this book, and many others, clanking around in my subconscious. I also felt that this new generation of young adults needed a book of their own rather than one borrowed from an earlier, older generation's coming of age. I was also looking for a way to reintroduce the truths of Western spirituality to the new multicultural world. And in this wobbly world since the World Trade Center attack, a realistic voice of encouragement needs to sound out.

What other symbols are in the book? Is there a secret code?
I have planted hundreds of symbols, in multiple layers, all over the book. Like hiding Easter eggs. You will never find them all. And I'm not going to tell you where they are. To start with, pay attention to numbers and names. Knowing your Bible helps a lot too.

Are you as into action sports as Josh is?
I'm afraid so. Half-pipe is my happy place. I live for stoke. A couple of times I have experienced his danger moments, personally, out in the waves. It's harrowing. I teach surfing in Orange County, California, and spend much of my winter at Big Bear, snowboarding too much. I wrote most of this book up there. I get cable just for one channel Fuel.tv. My favorite movie ever is *Second Thoughts* by local Huntington Beach surf film prodigy Timmy Turner. His family runs the Sugar Shack on Main Street, arguably the best place to get breakfast in the universe.

Are the themes of the story patterned on anything?
Yes. Paul of Tarsus writes: "If ye be led of the Spirit, ye are not under the law" (Galatians 5:18). I believe this is the whole reality around which the Bible rotates.

Who are your favorite authors?

They are mostly Dutch. Harry Mulisch. Thea Beckman. Cees Nooteboom. Maarten 't Hart. Geert Kimpen. I don't read a lot of English-language stuff. Mulisch's *Ontdekking van de Hemel* (*Discovery of Heaven*) may be the greatest novel ever written, but you kind of have to be Dutch to get it.

I also loved Steffen Kopetzky's *Grand Tour* (German) and share his passion for classic wristwatches. Steffen, if you're out there, come to California, and I'll teach you to surf.

As for theological writing, no one comes close to E. Stanley Jones. His *Victorious Living* (Summerside Press) is worth reading over and over for the rest of your life.

How do you see the book being used?

Primarily as a group or class study. High school students will get a lot more depth and hope out of it than from the dated classic *Catcher in the Rye,* and they may enjoy reading it. It would also make a good college text in an Intro to Religion class.

It would be especially good for book clubs (read the book all the way through together and then do the discussion questions) or youth groups (when led by an adult). The discussion questions have a level one (for younger age groups or those with a limited discussion time) and a level two (questions that take individuals and groups deeper).

Sunday morning junior high, senior high, or adult Sunday school classes may enjoy focusing on it for a few weeks.

Obviously, it's also fun to read on vacation in the sunshine all by yourself....

Why two main characters?

I wanted both a male and female perspective on growing up in our contemporary world. I also wanted to play them off of each other. Plus, as with two newscasters, you don't have to look at the same face the whole time.

Did things like the tar-and-feather scene (*pek en veren*) really happen in Europe after World War II?

Unfortunately, yes. This comes under the heading, if you want to look it up, of the "politics of retribution." Occupied countries often feel humiliated by their occupiers, and when the latter leave, there is an explosion of anger directed at those left behind who cooperated or collaborated with the invaders.

There was almost never any due process in these vigilante actions of retribution, and the singling out of those who were punished was done arbitrarily. Many collaborators escaped punishment altogether.

Researching this material is especially difficult because nations are ashamed, after coming to their senses, of this especially cruel and uncivilized retribution. So, for obvious reasons, they destroy and suppress the evidence of such incidents.

For (disturbing) photos of Dutch victims of retribution, please consider searching for photos under *Moffenmeiden* (Kraut girls). The most deeply disturbing ones have been removed from the Internet.

Please hear me: I did not choose the Hillegersberg location because of any evidence I have of such an event there; this book is totally a work of fiction. I chose the site because of its aesthetic beauty, which provides the ultimate contrast to the tar-and-feather scene.

I have attended the Hillegonda church there and had a profound experience of God's presence. I hope those from Hillegersberg who read the book will see the last scene in the book, which also takes place in their neighborhood, as the final word of restoration for postwar Europe. A Romans 8:28 moment.

It is almost impossible, for obvious reasons of the shame involved, to nail down actual times, places, and people involved in such widespread postwar events. A lot of pictures were taken of such events. And a lot of pictures were later burned by the owners when they fully realized what they had done.

For a serious book, it was written in very casual English. Why is that?

For the most part, the narrators are Kati and Josh, and at the climax of the book, they are only twenty-one years old. I did not want to put language to their thoughts that would not have integrity. I did clean up a little of their grammar, though.

The entire book is written in the casual register, much of it in first person.

Are you a Christian?

I don't like being vague about this. I am a committed follower of Jesus Christ and blessed to be a member of his Church. So, yes. I was raised in a wonderful Christian home and came to personal faith toward the end of college. I am part of the team leadership at RobinwoodChurch.com, and we have a worldwide podcast. You can tell from this novel that I have an abiding love for the Bible. That being said, I deeply love and cherish my friendships outside of my faith family. God loves all of us the same. When walls come down...

What languages do you speak? You seem to handle the European characters as a native would.

We are an international family. Wendy, my Dutch wife, was born and raised in Asia. Lars, my son, was born in Bonn, Germany. I was raised in the mountains of the American West. I speak fluent English. Dutch, and German and read the Bible in its original languages of Hebrew and Greek. Wendy's parents, who grew up in Rotterdam, suffered through the German occupation of Holland. They often had nothing to eat for days on end. Wendy's grandparents, who could no longer feed her father, sent him on an extended *hungertocht*, or "hunger trip," into the countryside to find food for himself. These all-too-common survival pilgrimages for little children, on their own, often lasted for months.

Josh and Kati do not get along with their parents. Do you, the author, have parent issues?

All humans have parent issues. But I am blessed to have been raised by outstanding parents in a loving, stable home. If you look carefully in the book, I identify more with the generation of the parents than with Josh and Kati. Look for pieces of my parents in the grandparents. When it comes to parenting, I am less satisfied with the job I did in parenting than the job my parents did. You can see some of that transparency in certain slivers of the book.

Are you optimistic or pessimistic about the future of the human race?

Militantly optimistic. With God's help, we will prevail. You will see some specifics about my optimism if you read the Zarzamora chapter of the epilogue carefully.

Will there be more books in this series?

Absolutely. Work with me on Twitter @RobinwoodChurch if you have ideas for the next volume.

What do you hope the reader will carry away after reading
The Blackberry Bush?

The realization that it's human to trap ourselves in broken responses to impossible demands. The awareness that there is a way out of this trap. You can be reborn onto a new path of life in the Spirit.

YOUR BACKSTORY

Your space to doodle, draw, scribble, think, and record insights....

Your Backstory

Your Backstory

Your Backstory

Your Backstory

ABOUT THE AUTHOR

DAVID HOUSHOLDER, Fulbright Scholar (University Bonn '88–'89) and international conference speaker, speaks three languages and earned his M.Div. at Chicago's Lutheran School of Theology. An avid philosophical-spiritual influencer, sponsored snowboarder, and surfing instructor at his home break, he enjoys tinkering on his '71 VW Bus. Currently he leads an indie-warehouse California beach-church, where he dreams and works for a better world. He has been happily married to Wendy for all of his adult life. They have raised one son together. They can't do life very well without cats around.

ThornHeart.com
RobinwoodChurch.com

Follow me on **Twitter @RobinwoodChurch**

also by DAVID HOUSHOLDER

"Open yourself up to the potent, awareness-changing presence of the Holy Spirit in your life. I've personally sat under Housholder's teaching on this topic."

—Ken Blanchard
The One Minute Manager

Have you ever watched "holy roller" preachers and felt like they're hosts of a party to which you weren't invited? Or, if you were invited, would you want to be? This unique guidebook for "normal" Christians who are curious about the whole "Holy Spirit" thing uses easy-to-understand language. Drawing on his own experience in both traditional Lutheran and Pentecostal churches, Housholder deftly bridges the gap between these two estranged camps, addressing topics such as: fluency in conversation about the Holy Spirit, who, or what, is the Holy Spirit, speaking in tongues, faith healings, the Word-Faith movement, prayer in the Spirit-filled life, and charismatic worship.

An engaging, boundary-breaking book that's a must-read.

Available from amazon and amazonkindle
Visit http://www.robinwoodchurch.com/podcast.html